ELUSIVE STAR

ELUSIVE STAR

Juliet Gray

Chivers Press • Thorndike Press
Bath, England Waterville, Maine USA

This Large Print edition is published by Chivers Press, England, and by Thorndike Press, USA.

Published in 2003 in the U.K. by arrangement with the author.

Published in 2003 in the U.S. by arrangement with Juliet Burton Literary Agency.

U.K. Hardcover   ISBN 0–7540–8827–8 (Chivers Large Print)
U.S. Softcover   ISBN 0–7862–4877–7 (Nightingale Series Edition)

The text of this Large Print edition is unabridged.
Other aspects of the book may vary from the original edition.

Set in 16 pt. New Times Roman.

Printed in Great Britain on acid-free paper.

British Library Cataloguing in Publication Data available

Library of Congress Control Number: 2002111675

CHAPTER ONE

He whistled softly to himself as the car sped along the dusty, country roads. The sun shone from a blue sky and the surrounding fields and hedges were green with the promise of Spring. It was a very hot day. The hood of the low-slung sports car was down and he appreciated the sunshine on his dark head and broad shoulders. His coat lay on the back seat together with his case and portable typewriter.

He whistled because he was content. His brief stay at the cottage had been peaceful and enjoyable: a sheaf of typescript in his case gave him a feeling of satisfaction. Even a faint reluctance to return to the bustle and noise and dirt of London could not destroy his mood of achievement.

A slow smile spread across his face and the whistle died. No doubt he would find a pile of work awaiting him at the office and a long list of appointments to be kept: his secretary would greet him with obvious relief; for the next few days, he would be beseiged by irate friends who had been left in the lurch by his sudden and unexpected decision to seek the solitude of his country cottage. He had woken one morning with an irresistible urge to get away from London and all the ties which bound him. He telephoned his office and informed his bewildered secretary that he was going down to the cottage, that all his appointments for the next two or three weeks must be cancelled. Then he threw the necessary things into a suit-case, enjoyed an immense breakfast, gave his man a holiday and walked out of the luxurious flat.

He drove away from the busy metropolis at full speed and headed south. For three weeks, he had not a care in the world; he had the ability to forget those things which he did not choose to remember for the time being; the quiet peace and beauty of the cottage had surrounded him and he was able to work undisturbed and with the knowledge that his work was satisfyingly brilliant.

Now it was finished. He was prepared to take up the old threads and return to the old way of life—until once more the need of solitude and the urge to write came upon him.

The car ate up the miles with ease. He switched on the radio and soft music floated out on to the warm air. It suited his mood.

He passed through a small village and caught sight of an attractive old inn—set back from the road—inviting. He did not refuse the invitation. He drove into the forecourt.

The beer quenched his thirst and washed away the dust of the roads from his throat. He leaned up against the bar and carried on a desultory conversation with the publican.

He was a striking figure. Tall, when he stood

up straight, his head almost touched the beams in the low bar. Broad-shouldered, narrow-waisted, lean-flanked—bronzed by many hours in the warm sun which had blessed the countryside for the past three weeks. Blue eyes of a brilliance which seemed to pierce the rather gloomy interior of the inn. He carried with him an air of magnetism—of charm—of culture. There was also warmth of personality which earned him many friends—true friends.

He returned to the car and went on his way.

The smooth-running engine suddenly caught and spluttered and a frown creased his brow. He slowed down and again the engine caught. His petrol gauge informed him that the tank was half-full. But he stopped and got out, pushed up the bonnet and investigated the engine. He soon found the fault but it was nothing he could remedy. A curse escaped his lips. Then he began to laugh softly. His car was apparently as reluctant as himself to return to London.

He looked about him. Green fields rolled away on both sides: the long road stretched before and beyond. The countryside was as beautiful and as desolate as any plain. In the far distance a low range of hills outlined the horizon.

He shrugged philosophically. Winding up the hood, he took his coat, locked the car and set off down the road at an easy pace with his coat slung over his shoulder. A passing car

3

would no doubt give him a lift to the nearest garage.

But it was a seldom used road and no cars made themselves visible to him. He walked on, enjoying the sunshine and the fresh air, glad of this last chance to fill his lungs, drinking in the beauty of the countryside.

He rounded a corner of the road and saw the house. It was a small, white house set back from the road—a narrow lane branched off towards it. It merged with the countryside and, despite its solitary position, did not look lonely. It had an immediate appeal for him and he turned from the road.

Bright curtains fluttered from open windows. The garden was neat and well-kept and a wooden swing had been fixed to an old tree. He pushed open the gate and walked up the path to the door. As he neared the house he heard the sound of a woman's voice raised in song—a bright, pleasant melody in keeping with its surroundings. He smiled as a nearby bird took up the melody, bursting into song. He was sensitive to atmosphere and as he paused by the door he felt an odd sensation, a tingling in his veins, a quickening of his heartbeats. He raised the heavy, old-fashioned knocker and banged it against the door.

He waited. The singing continued. He lifted the knocker again and a line from a long-forgotten poem ran through his thoughts—'Is there anyone there, asked the traveller . . .'

The door opened abruptly and he looked down at a young woman. He did not know what or whom he had expected but he felt a slight sense of shock.

She was young—that was his first impression. Her fair hair was dishevelled and ran wildly over her small, poised head. There was a smudge of flour on her cheek and a voluminous apron was tied about her slight body. She held a cloth on which she was wiping her hands. She raised inquiring eyes—eyes of a beauty so rare that he was astonished. They were clear and shining—the eyes of a happy woman—he felt himself drowning in their depths.

He pulled himself together. 'I'm sorry to bother you,' he said in his quiet, pleasant voice. 'My car's pegged out on me a little way down the road. I wondered if you had a telephone—or if you could direct me to the nearest garage?'

She smiled readily. 'Won't you come in?' She held the door open invitingly.

He hesitated a moment and then stepped into the cool interior of the house. He felt that he had crossed more than the threshold of a house.

She said, 'I thought you were a tradesman!' She lifted a hand and brushed back her unruly hair with a gesture that was filled with an odd grace. She led the way into a room and he followed without question. He noticed first the

5

sweet scent of flowers and then the aura of peace. He looked about the room appreciatively. It was large and furnished comfortably but a little shabbily. It gleamed in the sunshine, proof that the owner of the furniture loved and cared for it despite its shabbiness.

He said impulsively, 'What an attractive room!'

Her smile was enough thanks. 'I'm sorry about your car,' she said. 'Have you walked very far?'

He shrugged. 'A couple of miles—not more.'

'In this heat?' She said quickly, 'I've just made some tea—I'll get you some.' Before he could protest she slipped from the room, moving with an inborn grace that was so much a part of her.

He took out a cigarette and put it between his lips thoughtfully. The atmosphere of the room crept into his soul and he was at ease. Suddenly he realized that his feelings were imbued with a sense of having come home— this was odd indeed for a man who had never known a home—who had never had any roots; he had merely existed through the years in different surroundings without calling any of them 'home'. Even the cottage, which he loved and needed, lacked the complete and welcoming warmth of this house. He felt a new emotion—envy. It was unexpected and

6

startling for he had never regretted his lack of anything—he had never admitted that he lacked anything—he had always been entirely self-sufficient and glad of his freedom. Yet he envied the owner of this house and he found it possible in his heart to envy the man who could call such a sensitive and beautiful woman his wife!

She came back into the room carrying a tray which she placed on the table by the window. He took the cup of tea from her with a word of thanks.

'I'm afraid we haven't a telephone,' she said. At that moment, a small boy ran past the window. She put her head through the open window and called him by name. He stopped and came back. 'Michael, will you cycle into the village and tell Bert Stoner that a car has broken down two miles up the road from here. Tell him it's urgent.'

The boy nodded, grinned impishly and ran off again.

She turned back into the room. 'It won't take him very long,' she said, 'and he'll welcome the chance of riding back in Bert's lorry. Michael loves cars and all to do with them.'

'How old is he?' he asked.

'Ten—he's small for his age,' she replied.

He felt a shock of surprise. She looked so young—too young to be the mother of a ten year old son. He studied her face—was it

7

deceptively youthful and innocent?

'This is very good of you,' he said. 'There really wasn't any need to send your son—if you'd given me directions I would have found the village.'

A rich, amused smile touched her lips. 'Michael isn't my son,' she said quickly. 'He's my young brother.'

Confusion swept through him. 'I'm sorry . . .' he began.

She looked down at herself and her expression was rueful as she regarded the voluminous apron, the sleeves of her dress rolled up above the elbows, the smears of flour on her forearms.

'Please don't apologize,' she said. 'I'm very much the housewife, I'm afraid.'

He looked at her slim, beautiful hands and noted the absence of any wedding ring. Sudden relief flooded him. So she did not belong to any man. He did not analyse the sense of relief.

He heard no sound but she turned her head quickly and then hurried towards the door. 'Excuse me,' she said. 'My sister is calling me.' Once again she slipped from the room.

He walked over to the window. The boy wheeled his cycle down the path towards the gate; sensing the man's gaze, he turned and grinned impishly at him. He was small for his age but wiry and suntanned—auburn hair rioted over the boy's head and gleamed in the

8

sunlight. He mounted the bicycle and set off down the lane. A piercing whistle floated back on the summer breeze and the man smiled involuntarily at the sound. Curiosity stirred in him. Who were these people? Why did they choose to live in such a solitary spot? Where were their parents?

It seemed a long time before the woman returned. She looked a little flushed and he noted how it enhanced her natural, unadorned beauty. Her eyes seemed brighter than ever.

'I didn't mean to leave you so long,' she said. 'Would you like to come out into the garden and sit in the sun until Michael gets back? My sister wants to meet you.' Again the hint of colour in her cheeks and he wondered at it. She went on hastily, 'We're rather out of touch here—we don't see many people and Lisa gets a little lonely at times.' She added quietly, 'My sister is an invalid, you see, so she's tied very much to the house and garden.'

He felt a swift rush of sympathy. He stubbed his cigarette and turned towards her. 'I should like to meet your sister,' he said warmly. 'I must introduce myself—I should have done so before. My name is Desmond Crane.' He said it with a certain pride for it was a famous name but there was no flicker of recognition in her eyes. He felt a sense of disappointment.

She smiled. 'I'm Isobel Lomax.'

She put out a hand and he took it between his strong, brown fingers. A slight pressure on

9

his part then she took her hand away.

He followed her along the passage to the back of the house and they stepped through a door on to a stone terrace which had evidently been added to the original building. A wheelchair was drawn close to the edge of the terrace. A table and two wicker-work chairs stood beside it.

Desmond paused and the girl in the chair turned her head, her expression eager and intense. He caught his breath. He had expected a child but this was a woman—a small, fragile and beautiful woman. The delicate bones of her lovely face were etched clearly under the pallor of the skin. Her hair was the colour of ripe corn and it fell about her face in a sheet of rich silk. Her smile was almost ethereal. He knew immediately that this was a woman who had suffered and come to terms with pain; a woman who had learned to accept all that life brought to her without complaint or question; a woman who was sensitive and good and possessed of an innocent purity which shone from her eyes. A woman who loved life and was eager to know more of it.

Isobel smiled at her sister and drew Desmond forward. 'This is Desmond Crane,' she said. She looked up at him. 'My sister, Melissa—but everyone calls her Lisa.'

Lisa's hand was tremulous in his grasp and his pressure was gentle. She smiled. 'Sheer coincidence? Or are you the writer and publisher?'

'The very same,' he admitted. He drew up a chair and sat down beside her, feeling very much at his ease. 'My sins always find me out,' he said.

'Is it a sin to be well-known?' she countered.

'I sometimes think so.'

Isobel paused a moment and then said, 'I'll leave you two to talk, if you don't mind, Mr. Crane. I'm in the middle of baking . . .

He rose instinctively and with a quick smile she was gone. He resumed his seat and turned to Lisa Lomax.

'Isobel was telling me about your car,' she said. 'A stroke of luck for us—but annoying for you, I expect.'

'Not at all. I was on my way back to London—very reluctantly. This is by way of being a reprieve.'

'I've never been to London,' she admitted. 'I've always wanted to see it—but it sounds as though you don't like it, Mr. Crane.'

'I love the place,' he assured her readily, 'but sometimes I feel the need to get away from it. It can be very overwhelming.' He went on, 'I've been staying at my cottage in Fairfield—it's the only place where I can write.'

'And have you been writing?' she wanted to know.

He nodded. 'Yes. Into the small hours of the

11

night—getting a new novel off my chest. Now, it's finished and duty calls, I'm afraid.' He grinned. 'I shall find a desk heaped with work when I get back to my office.' He was relieved that she had made no mention of his other books. Admiration was always appreciated but it could sometimes be tedious—and so often he had to listen to the usual flattering comments on this or that book from people who tried to impress upon him how qualified they were to judge.

He looked into the garden—as neat and well-kept as the one at the front of the house. Flowers grew in profusion, colourful, sweet-scented and very lovely. An apple tree was in full blossom. The summer dress which Lisa wore was the identical colouring of the blossom—a blend of pink and white, soft and delicate. He brought out his cigarettes and offered the slim, gold case to the woman at his side. She shook her head and he helped himself.

'Have you always lived here?' he asked after a moment. Then he told himself that he already knew the answer—they were as much a part of the house as the aura of quiet contentment and peace which he sensed.

She nodded. 'We were all born here—Isobel, Michael and myself. My parents came here when they were married.' Her expression was suddenly clouded. 'My mother died when Michael was born—my father a year later.

They were very much in love and he was lost without her—after she died, he never again put brush to canvas—he was an artist, Mr. Crane. You may have heard of Nigel Lomax.'

'Of course I have,' Desmond said quickly. Now he knew why the white and gold beauty of this woman was familiar to him. He recalled the painting which had made Nigel Lomax well known in the art world—'Portrait of Laura'— the portrait of his wife. Lisa resembled her mother very much. There was the same air of innocence, of natural goodness, of purity of spirit and of fragility—a fragility which in Lisa's case owed some of its being to her physical handicap. He frowned a little. She was too beautiful to be tied to a wheelchair, to have to content herself with so little of life, to be denied the pleasures and joys and happiness of other women of her age.

She said suddenly, 'You're wondering how long I have been confined to this wheelchair?' He was taken aback by her swift insight into his thoughts. 'I was born paralysed,' she said quietly. 'I've never walked a step in my life.'

'Can nothing be done?' He felt a swift rush of sympathy through his entire being.

'Nothing. When I was a child I saw all the specialists—I think they were rather baffled by my case but they all agreed that I could never hope to walk, to lead an active life.' There was an odd note of finality in her voice.

'But you've learnt to live with that

13

knowledge, haven't you?' It was a statement rather than a question.

She nodded. 'Yes, of course. I'm not bitter about it—not now.' She smiled her singularly sweet smile. 'Bitterness is rather a futile emotion, don't you think, Mr. Crane.'

'How old are you?' he asked abruptly.

There was no flicker of surprise in her lovely eyes. 'Twenty-one,' she replied evenly.

'So young?' He was thinking that she was very young to have learnt this lesson—but she was not a normal woman of twenty-one—pain and helplessness had matured her beyond her years. His gaze was attracted to a small, neat book which lay on the table. It was a children's book with a brightly illustrated cover. He picked it up and turned it over idly in his hands.

'That isn't an example of my taste in literature,' she said quickly, and a laugh bubbled to her lips.

He read the title and then his interest was caught. He said, 'Lomax? Any connection?'

'Isobel wrote the stories—I merely illustrated them.' She smiled at him. 'It all began five years ago. Isobel wanted me to have a new interest. She persuaded me to take up sketching again—it was a hobby of mine when I was a little girl—and she asked me to illustrate a few stories she'd scribbled.' As she spoke, he skimmed through the pages, pausing occasionally at a particularly pretty or

14

colourful sketch, reading a word here and there. 'We decided to try our luck with a publisher—but we had very little hope of success.'

'This isn't the first?'

'No. We've done several between us now—it provides the jam for our bread and butter.'

He nodded. 'I'm sure that Hawtrey gives you a fair deal,' he said lightly. 'We don't specialize in books for children otherwise I'd ask you to submit your next manuscript to us.'

'Oh, we have a contract with Hawtrey,' she said quickly. 'As for a fair deal—well, we've no complaints.'

They went on to discuss books in general and he was surprised to find that she was extremely well-read. On second thoughts, he decided that reading was probably her main interest while all other active interests were out of the question. They spoke of art and she proved to be very knowledgeable—whether through instinct or through tuition from her father, he knew not. Music too was discussed and her eyes shone as he told her of concerts he had attended at the Festival Hall or at the Albert Hall, certain composers he had met or particularly admired. He could talk at great length on music and his knowledge was widespread. He found it easy to talk to this young woman who listened with keen interest, her lips slightly parted, her eyes bright and intelligent, her occasional comments proving

15

that she understood and assimilated his words.

Isobel slipped out to them once but finding them deep in conversation and apparently engrossed in each other, she turned quietly and went back into the house. They did not notice her come and go.

It seemed a very short time before Michael was back with the garage mechanic. His cycle was slung into the back of the lorry and Michael was sitting proudly alongside Bert Stoner, chattering away brightly.

He jumped down from the cab of the lorry as Isobel came to the door, attracted by the sound of the engine as it chugged slowly down the narrow lane. She waved a hand to the mechanic and then hurried through the house to tell their unexpected visitor that the breakdown lorry was on the scene.

Desmond looked up as she came out.

'Michael is back with the car mechanic,' she told him.

He rose to his feet, feeling a strange reluctance to leave the pleasant, peaceful house, 'Then I must show him where the car is,' he said slowly. He gave his hand to Lisa. 'I hope we'll meet again,' he said. 'I've enjoyed our conversation very much.'

She smiled up at him, her eyes warm. 'Perhaps you'll visit us again, Mr. Crane. You'll be very welcome.' At her sister's words, Isobel caught her breath slightly and a slight flush stained her cheeks. There was no mistaking the blatant invitation and she wondered if Desmond Crane would resent Lisa's apparent interest in him. She glanced swiftly at him and found him smiling.

'May I come again?' he asked Isobel quietly, 'I should very much like to visit you both. You've been very kind to a complete stranger.' He did not add that he had never felt less like a stranger in his life where this house and these two women were concerned.

He climbed into the cab of the lorry and gave the mechanic a word of thanks for coming so promptly. He told him roughly where the car waited and his own idea of the fault. Bert Stoner let in the clutch and the lorry began to roll slowly down the lane.

Desmond looked back and lifted a hand in brief salute. He looked at the boy who was swinging backwards and forwards on the wooden gate, his copper curls a bright streak of colour, his small face lit by an impish, expansive grin. He looked at the woman who stood in the doorway of the house, still wrapped in the voluminous apron, her fair hair framing her sweetly innocent face, a smile just lifting the corners of her mouth, yet he had the impression that her beautiful eyes were very serious at this moment. He looked at the small white house with its open windows and welcoming appearance—and he knew that before long he would be back. He knew that he could not stay away. Something about the place drew a chord of response in him and his interest was stirred very deeply by the Lomax family . . .

CHAPTER TWO

Isobel watched until a bend in the lane hid the lorry and its occupants from sight. Then a little sigh escaped her and she recognized the emotion that touched her as disappointment. Her eyes were suddenly bright, startled.

She called to her brother and he leaped from the gate and ran towards her. Michael never seemed to do anything slowly. He was always swift and energetic: all his movements seemed to be impulsive rather than controlled.

'I'm just going to get the tea—hadn't you better wash?' she asked automatically.

'There's a streak of flour on your cheek,' he merely replied with the candour of small boys. 'And your hair is in an awful mess, too—what have you been doing?'

'Baking cakes for you to eat,' she retorted and rumpled his hair. They went into the house together and Michael slipped an affectionate hand into her arm. He was a demonstrative child but a lonely one. So many years separated him from his sisters and there were few children in the neighbourhood whose company he sought. It was his one ambition to go away to school: not so much because he wanted to leave his home for he was happy there and he loved his sisters; he felt the need for the companionship of boys of his own age and interests. In a strangely adult way, he knew that the education he received from the village school was far below his capacity for knowledge. But he was a sensible boy and once Isobel had explained to him that they could not afford school fees for him, he philosophically accepted the fact and applied himself with fresh industry to his school work and to the books he loved so much. He was an inveterate reader and Lisa encouraged him in this. Nearly all the money which she received as her share in their earnings from the books she and Isobel produced between them was spent on Michael. She sent off for books for him, indulged all his boyish hobbies—model aeroplanes, stamp collections and such.

They lived very happily together. They were poor for Nigel Lomax had left little but the house: he painted mostly for his own pleasure and sold few of his works. Many of them were hung in the house to this day.

Isobel was devoted to her sister and Michael. She was completely selfless and never complained of their lack of money. She grew their vegetables and some fruit: she baked bread and cakes and pies; she kept the house spotless and the garden neat. They had little entertainment but that of their own making.

Isobel made most of her own clothes and some of Lisa's: she washed and ironed, sewed and darned, cooked and cleaned. She had brought Michael up from infancy and was more mother than sister to the boy. If she ever dreamed her youthful dreams and longed for love, a home and family of her own, there was no mention of it.

Isobel prepared tea while Michael washed his face and hands. Burying his face in the towel, he demanded indistinctly, 'Who was that man, Isobel?'

Deftly spreading newly-baked bread, she replied, 'Just a traveller. His name was Desmond Crane.'

'Where was he going?'

'Back to London, I believe. If you want to know any more about him, you'd better ask Lisa. She was talking to him—I was too busy.'

She carried the tea-tray out to the terrace. Lisa was sitting very still, her hands idle in her lap, her eyes very bright as she gazed over the garden. 'He was very nice,' she said suddenly as Isobel laid the tea-things on the table. 'I wonder if we will see him again.'

'I expect he's a very busy man,' Isobel replied. 'He will have forgotten us by the time he gets back to London—ships that pass in the night, Lisa.'

'I don't think he will forget,' her sister said slowly. Michael came out of the house and sat down at the table. Isobel poured tea and

20

placed Lisa's cup near to her hand. Then she sat down and stirred her tea idly. She toyed with food but ate very little. For some reason, she had no appetite. It was still very hot in the garden. She had taken off the apron to reveal a cool green summer dress. She had hastily run a comb through her hair and wiped the flour from her cheek.

Now she said lightly, 'I expect he thought I was the daily woman—he certainly thought I was Michael's mother.' She laughed, 'I can't blame him—I always look rather harassed on baking day!'

Michael said abruptly, 'Why didn't he stay to tea? Was he in a hurry to get away? Bert could have fixed the car and brought it here.'

Lisa and Isobel exchanged glances. 'I never thought of asking him,' Isobel said slowly. She poured fresh tea for herself. 'What did you two talk about all that time?' she asked brightly.

'Books, for one thing. Music—and art. He's very interesting, Isobel—he knows so much.' She sighed a little.

Isobel looked at her sharply. Lisa was always so contented. She hoped that Desmond Crane had not fired her vivid imagination with talk of unknown things which would make her restless and impatient with her lot. Later that evening, when Michael had gone to bed, the two young women sat in the cool sitting-room. A radio issued soft music from one corner of the room. Isobel sat with a pile of Michael's socks in her lap, darning busily, her slender fingers nimbly plying the needle. Lisa held her sketch-book and pencil but she was not using them with her usual industry. She was very quiet.

A strain of music caused Lisa to lift her head sharply. She listened for a moment then a smile flickered about her mouth. She said slowly, 'Mr. Crane told me that this was one of his favourites—it is lovely, isn't it, Isobel?'

Isobel laid down the sock she was darning. A stab of fear shot through her being. 'You liked him very much, didn't you?' she asked quietly.

Lisa nodded. 'Didn't you?'

'Yes—but we don't know anything about him, Lisa. We'll probably never see him again—don't weave dreams about him, darling.' She knew that her words had reached home by the sudden tilt of her sister's chin. Lisa had met so few men in her life—never a man as handsome, as fascinating, as interesting as Desmond Crane.

She was glad that the knocker resounded through the house at that moment. She rose from her chair.

'That's Frank,' Lisa said, but she had caught her breath sharply at the sound. Her words held a faint trace of disappointment.

Frank Cummins was their nearest neighbour. He owned a farm which was fairly successful and he had known the Lomax family

22

all their lives. He followed Isobel into the low, cool sitting-room and instantly the large room seemed somewhat smaller. He was very tall and extremely broad. His muscles rippled beneath the coloured shirt and grey trousers which he wore. His hair was bleached by the sun until it was almost white, making a startling contrast to the ruddy, glowing skin of his pleasant face. White teeth flashed as he greeted Lisa. He was a welcome and familiar figure in that house and he was a good friend to them. He was dependable, steady and reliable, blessed with many good qualities—and he loved Isobel with a deep, warm love which had lasted now for a good many years. But there was a deep core of shyness in his nature and his love had always remained unspoken.

He held a book in his hand which he offered to Lisa. 'I went over to Hanleigh to-day,' he said in his deep, hearty voice. 'Here's that book you wanted.'

She took it eagerly. 'Thank you, Frank—how good you are.' She did not doubt that he had made a special journey in order to obtain the book which they had discussed the other evening. Frank was that type of man.

He threw himself into a comfortable armchair which gave under his weight. He was a big man and it was all solid bone and muscle. He relaxed and yawned widely. Taking out his pipe, he began to fill it from his pouch.

'This is very pleasant,' he said as he said so often when he came over to spend a few hours with the two women.

Isobel smiled at him. 'I'll put the kettle on,' she said, and went from the room.

'Young Michael in bed?' Frank asked a moment later. 'I saw him haring into the village on his bike this afternoon—I ought to overhaul that machine for him, you know. It's getting very decrepit.'

'We had a visitor,' Lisa said slowly. She felt reluctant to share the experience even with Frank. 'A car broke down and its owner came here for help. Isobel sent Michael to Stoner's garage for the breakdown lorry.'

He nodded. 'I was talking to Bert in the village just now—I heard all about it. He was quite taken with the chap—more likely because of the fat tip he got rather than the man's personality!' He chuckled.

Isobel came back into the room. 'Have you had a busy day, Frank? You look rather weary this evening.'

'I'm always busy at this time of the year,' he replied easily. 'But if I look tired, it's because I was up all last night. Sunshine had trouble calving—oh, she's all right now. Lovely twin calves—black as the ace of spades, the pair of 'em. But they gave me a devil of a time of it last night.' He flashed his broad smile at her. 'But a cup of your tea will soon put me to rights, Isobel. We were just talking about that

24

chap whose car broke down—lucky for him you were so near and that Michael had his bike. If he's a city chap, he wouldn't have liked the three-mile walk to the village!' He grinned.

'He walked two miles here,' Lisa told him. 'He said he was glad of the exercise. He was very nice, Frank—so easy to talk to . . .' She broke off.

Frank winked at Isobel. 'We'll have to keep an eye on our Lisa,' he said jovially. 'Seems like this chap made quite an impression—he'll probably be back to thank you for your help. Lisa's a pretty girl!'

'For all we know, he's a married man,' Isobel said, more sharply than she intended.

'But he isn't,' Lisa said. 'I asked him.'

Isobel could not repress a laugh. 'I hope he appreciated your interest!'

'He didn't seem to mind at all.' Lisa addressed Frank. 'His name is Desmond Crane—the writer, you know.'

Frank looked a trifle blank. 'Is he well known?'

Lisa chuckled. 'Apparently not—the name doesn't mean anything to you!'

He shrugged. 'I'm not a reader, Lisa—you know that. I don't get much time for books.'

The next two hours passed pleasantly. Frank was not a great conversationalist but his presence was very comforting and the girls liked to have him at the house. He spent two or three evenings a week with them and never failed to bring something with him—a book for Lisa, or a bunch of wild flowers for Isobel, a scarf or a piece of cheap jewellery he had picked up in the nearby big town, a present for Michael—sweets or comics or a set of new stamps.

When he left, Isobel went to the door with him. He took her hand and pressed it between his own big fingers. His hands were broad and massive and strangely gentle—a touch could calm a cow in pain or quieten an angry horse. He had a way with animals, sensing instinctively their need—but he was clumsy with this woman he loved with every fibre of his being.

She looked up at the sky with its bright stars and dark velvet cloak of night. 'It's a beautiful night, Frank,' she said quietly.

Unexpectedly, he replied, quoting softly, '"*She walks in beauty like the night*"—that's nice, isn't it, Isobel? Something I remember from my schooldays.' He looked down at her small hand resting in his. He grinned a little sheepishly. 'I'm not much good at quoting poetry—I'm a farmer and a pig-breeder. The two don't go together.'

'Yes, they do, Frank. There's poetry in farming—in tilling the land and sowing the harvest—in bringing new life into the world.'

'I suppose so—but I could never put it into words the way you do.' He added abruptly, 'What did you think of that chap, Isobel?'

She was a little surprised. 'I don't know that I gave him much thought—I was in the middle of baking, He seemed very nice—he was very polite, anyway.' She gave a little laugh. 'We're so far apart from the world here that a strange man can upset the whole village—I suppose everyone was talking about him tonight?'

He nodded. 'Yes, they were. Well, I must go—perhaps I'll have a peaceful night for a change. I'll see you tomorrow, Isobel . . .' He looked at her quickly. 'You haven't forgotten that you promised to go into Hanleigh with me tomorrow?'

She had forgotten but she said quickly, 'No, of course not. Pick me up at three o'clock, will you?'

He nodded. 'Good night, then . . .'

'Good night, Frank.' She withdrew her hand.

She waited until he closed the garden gate behind him and set off down the lane, then she went into the house and closed the door.

Lisa looked up as she entered the sitting-room.

'You were a long time. Don't tell me that Frank actually popped the question at last?'

Isobel smiled and shook her head. 'I still think you're wrong, darling. If Frank wanted to marry me, he'd have said so long ago—besides, I don't want to get married. I'm perfectly happy as I am—and I have you and Michael to consider.'

A shadow crossed her sister's face. 'It's all wrong,' she said slowly. 'You're twenty-four and it's time you thought about marriage. I know it's out of the question for me but I've resigned myself to that. But you—Isobel, you deserve to be happy.' She paused and then added: 'Would you marry Frank if he asked you?'

'No.' The answer was definite but low.

'Because of us.' It was a statement not a question.

'I don't love Frank. I'm very fond of him and he's a good friend. But one doesn't marry for friendship's sake, Lisa.' She scanned her sister's face. 'Why all this talk of marriage, darling? It's never worried either of us before.'

'It's worried me for a long time but I haven't mentioned it,' Lisa retorted. 'It's all wrong,' she repeated. 'You never meet any men or go out on dates—what chance have you of ever falling in love and getting married?'

Isobel crossed over to her sister's wheelchair and smoothed the long, silken mass from Lisa's face. 'I've no wish to meet any men,' she said quietly. She smiled. 'I'm going out with Frank tomorrow—isn't that a date? As for falling in love, there's plenty of time for that, Lisa. I'm only twenty-four, after all.' She tilted Lisa's chin with a gentle hand. 'Darling, you must have thought about getting married—are you bitter?'

Lisa shook her head. 'Not in the slightest.

28

Or rather, not now. When I was younger, I used to dream of a handsome lover arriving unexpectedly on the doorstep and carrying me off to London.' A rather lovely, very sweet smile touched her lips. 'I used to tell myself that love would work miracles—that I would be able to get out of this chair and walk for the man I loved. But now I know that I shall never meet my handsome lover and I shall never marry. No man would want a helpless wife— and I wouldn't burden any man even if he wanted me.'

Isobel bent her head and touched the smooth cheek with her lips. 'I shall never marry while you need me, my Lisa—we'll be two old maids together in our little house and we'll be so happy.'

Lisa raised her hand and touched the fair head so close to her own. 'I'm tired,' she said quietly. 'Let's go to bed, Isobel.'

Isobel lay between the cool sheets in her little room above Lisa's. Her eyes were open and she gazed into the darkness, her gentle heart troubled. The two sisters had never talked of love and marriage before. It was a subject that seemed to hold no promise for either of them. Yet today . . . had the advent of Desmond Crane anything to do with it, Isobel wondered. He was a very handsome man and his charm had filled the house with its presence. It was not surprising if he had stirred Lisa's young and innocent heart.

She was filled with pity for her sister—sweet and uncomplaining Lisa who was fully aware of the knowledge that life could hold no promise of fulfilment for her yet bitterness never touched her soul and she welcomed every new day without resenting the fact that each day was very much like the last.

If only there was something she could do for Lisa. All her life she had talked of going to London—but the expense and the journey had prevented it. Her life was filled with the books she loved so much, her natural gift for drawing which she had inherited from their father but which lacked the genius of his work, her enjoyment of the countryside and the varying seasons, her interest in Michael and his education . . .

Isobel twisted and turned in her small bed, the gentle night breeze fluttering the curtains at the open window, the moonbeams dancing on the ceiling. She watched them and a smile touched her lips. If only they could catch the moonbeams and find them turn to silver in their fingers. Her thoughts ran on . . . Money was the drawback. There had always been so little of it—yet they had been happy. Content with their simple life—yet dreaming of the world they did not know. A world where the promise of living seemed to attract them. An enchanted fairyland to which money was the key. She had never been in a position to work for a living. She could not leave Lisa and

Michael to fend for themselves. The success of their little books had been a godsend. It enabled them to live simply but happily. But if she had real wealth . . . Lisa could go to London and to all the other places which were merely names to them—enchanting names— names which caught the imagination. Michael could go to a good school where his excellent brain would gladly absorb the knowledge he longed to gain. She could accompany Lisa on her travels, look after her, protect her from the dangers which the road might offer. There would be lovely clothes to buy for Lisa— clothes which had been talked about and bought on imaginary shopping expeditions to famous London shops or Paris salons. They would go to theatres and art galleries, museums and exhibitions . . . they would meet people like Desmond Crane, interesting and intelligent, experienced, pleasant and charming . . . Desmond Crane, handsome, tall and well-spoken, handsome and wealthy . . .

At this point, her eyes closed and she slept to dream—a confused, exciting and strangely disturbing dream in which Desmond Crane figured prominently as the man who brought to her feet the riches which enabled her to do all she wanted to do for Lisa and Michael.

In her room below, Lisa lay wakeful for a long time—long after her sister slept. She cradled her smooth cheek on a slim hand and the soft, silken mass of her lovely hair fell across the cool pillows. Her slim, beautiful and helpless body lay still beneath the covers— long, useless legs which were thin because of wasted muscles.

Frank Cummins had spoken more truthfully than he realized. Desmond Crane had made quite an impression on her vulnerable emotions. She could visualize so clearly his tall, powerful body, the handsome, bronzed face, the proud dark head. She felt again the slight shock which had stirred her slim body when his brilliant blue eyes had looked down at her with apparent admiration in their depths. She could not recall very much of their conversation for she had listened more to the music of his pleasant voice than to the words he uttered. The magnetism of his charm had attracted and surrounded her. His departure had left her with a sense of physical loss and she knew that it was vital that she should see him again. She knew also without analysing her certainty that she would see him again.

She compared him with Frank. Dear Frank—so thoughtful and kind, powerful and manly yet gentle. She had known him all her life—could not remember a time when he had not been a part of her life. His devotion to Isobel was strangely touching yet his inherent shyness prevented him from speaking of it to her. Not that there was really any need. Isobel was as aware of it as Lisa. A woman always knows when a man loves her. But because

Isobel did not want to hurt Frank, she would not give him encouragement to speak. Lisa knew that her sister would never marry Frank although she had a very great affection for him. A slight frown touched her brow. Isobel would never marry while she had Michael and herself to consider, Lisa knew. She had known before Isobel put it into words. If only there were some way to free her sister of the burden which was herself. Isobel was being denied her natural instincts—so was Lisa but this did not cross her mind.

Because she was sensitive to her sister's thoughts and moods, Lisa knew that Isobel's reaction to Desmond Crane was one of fear. Fear that he would disturb the even tenor of their contentment. Fear that Lisa had formed too swift and impulsive a liking for him. Fear that he had aroused the first faint stirrings of emotions which could never know fulfilment.

Lisa was very honest with herself. She admitted that he had indeed brought thoughts and feelings to the surface which had always been carefully suppressed or barely acknowledged. His unexpected intrusion into their lives was the first ripple on the calm waters of contentment. But Lisa knew that she would not have it otherwise. She was glad that her heart sang with the thoughts of him and the blood flowed swifter in her veins because she had met Desmond Crane. She did not look into the future. The present happiness was

33

sufficient.

Her dreams were untroubled and very sweet. She walked hand in hand with the man she loved along the banks of a gently flowing river and Isobel was left behind, smiling, standing at the door of the little white house . . .

CHAPTER THREE

Desmond Crane broke off. His secretary, startled by the abrupt cessation of his quiet, smooth dictation, looked up with a gleam of inquiry in her intelligent eyes, pencil poised over her note-book.

He looked at her with unseeing eyes. His mind had suddenly left the cool, rather austere room with its black, contemporary office furniture—winging back to the little white house tucked off the country road, fifty miles from London. The memory of it had been with him for the last two days—not only the vision of the house where it stood in secluded peace surrounded by the green fields and the colour of the well-kept garden—but also the two young women. A line of a poem kept running through his mind—'of fair and shining beauty.' To him these few words symbolized Isobel and Lisa Lomax. They were beautiful with more than superficial fairness—purity of spirit and

34

goodness of heart seemed to shine from their lovely eyes and permeate their very beings. He did not seek to analyse the deep impression the house and its occupants had made on him. He simply knew that he meant to return.

Before he left the small village, he had made an inquiry as to the address of the white house. On his return to London, his first action was to order bouquets to be sent to the two young women. A little smile quirked his lips now as he thought of their surprised pleasure at the unexpected gesture. To each bouquet had been attached one of his cards with a little message:

With thanks for your kindness to a passing traveller.

Linda Holly noted the smile and the sudden warmth in his eyes. She wondered where his thoughts had wandered.

Suddenly he returned to the present. 'I'm sorry, Linda,' he said. 'Would you read back that last paragraph—I've lost the thread.' The letter completed, he smiled at her and said: 'That's all for now. You can go to lunch, Linda.'

She rose and closed her note-book. 'You have an appointment with Mr. Francis at three, sir.' She knew that she reminded him unnecessarily for he had an excellent memory.

He nodded. 'I'm going out now but I shall be back by then.' He got to his feet and walked over to the window. He looked down on the busy London square below. A taxi pulled up before the big white building and his eyes narrowed a little as he recognized the woman who stepped out on to the pavement below. There was no mistaking that tall, exquisitely slim figure or the poised, raven head. Over his shoulder he said quickly, 'Ring down and tell Harris that I'm on my way. It will save Miss Fairfax a journey.'

He did not wait for the lift. He ran lithely down the wide staircase and found Helen waiting for him, talking to the porter with the easy charm she so readily expended, be it duke or dustman.

Desmond strode to her side and touched her elbow. 'For once I'm punctual,' he said lightly.

She turned and looked him over slowly, her eyes finally warming as they met his. 'You look very fit, Desmond. Country life suits you.'

He smiled. 'Unfortunately, business prevents me from enjoying it all the time. Shall we go? My car is parked in the square.'

They sauntered out of the building into the bright sunlight. She smiled up at him. 'I should be very angry with you,' she said lightly. 'You ruined two of my dinner parties by your absence—and theatre tickets for the new musical were wasted.'

'But you aren't angry with me,' he countered. 'You never are—not for very long, at least.'

'I am until I see you,' she replied.

'Surely you found someone to take my place?'

'You would be the first one to call that impossible, my dear Desmond,' she told him. 'There is only one Desmond Crane, after all—my parties fell very flat without you.'

'I'm sorry, Helen—but London is no place for me when genius burns.'

She nodded. 'I quite understood, really, my dear. But it was a little disconcerting.' She linked her hand in his arm. 'However, you're back now for a while, I hope, so perhaps I can count on your support at the Marden dinner-party next week?'

He grimaced. 'My God—must we, Helen?'

'I'm afraid so. Their eldest daughter has finally caught a man—so big celebrations are in order. The dinner-party is only the beginning...'

They reached the car and Desmond slid into the driving seat after helping Helen into her seat. He turned on the ignition and released the clutch.

'I've booked a table at the Naylor,' he said. 'Suit you?' She nodded and the car drew slowly away from the kerb and nosed its way into the stream of traffic.

Desmond leaned back and exhaled blue-grey cigarette smoke from his nostrils. They had eaten a good meal and the conversation had been light and pleasant. Helen was excellent company, intelligent, witty and amusing. He smiled across the table at her, invoking a quick response of warmth to her eyes and lips. It struck him very forcibly that she was a beautiful woman. He had known her for several years but it suddenly seemed to him that he had never looked at her loveliness with such vivid clarity. Blue-black hair which she wore swept back from her wide, intelligent brow in a sophisticated short cut: magnolia white skin that was almost transparent; straight, narrow nose and lips that were etched with incredible fineness; eyes of such a deep blue that they seemed bottomless, fringed with long black lashes; a proud chin and exquisite bone formation of her lovely face. She was magnificent. Her tall, slender body was the admiration of her dressmakers and she wore beautiful clothes. Everything about her was elegant and expensive from the tip of her well-groomed head to the toes of her fashionable pointed shoes. Her slim hands were manicured to perfection. Helen Fairfax was the darling of society and she was popular with everyone who knew her. The daughter of wealthy parents, she had known an expensive education and every whim had been gratified but she remained the most unspoilt person that Desmond had ever known. There was no trace of the snob in her person. The only fault he had ever found with Helen was her impetuosity where men were concerned but this he considered to be none of his business. It often puzzled him that at twenty-eight she was still unmarried but whenever he teased her on the subject, she merely said that she had never met the man who was worthy of her—this with an amused gleam in her eye. He sometimes thought that she was possessed of too independent a spirit for marriage. It did not occur to him that there was only one man she wanted to marry—and he seemed completely blind to the fact.

She raised a quizzical eyebrow. 'There's a look in your eyes which disturbs me, my dear. What are you thinking about?'

He said with his innate candour: 'I was thinking what a very beautiful woman you are, Helen.'

There was a momentary pause born of surprise. Then she said lightly: 'Thank you. Compliments from you are totally unexpected.'

He grinned. 'I'm not the type of man who bestows compliments lightly, am I?'

'Which makes them all the more sincere,' she said quietly. She leaned forward suddenly. 'What happened while you were away, Desmond?'

It was his turn to be surprised. 'What happened? I don't understand you, my dear.'

'You're different,' she said. 'I can't define it but there's something about you which wasn't there three weeks ago. It isn't just the writing you've done at the cottage—I know the air of satisfaction and contentment you bring back with you on such occasions. What is it, my dear Desmond?' There was a great warmth in her voice, a quiet gentleness which touched him.

He thought for a long moment. It was not the first time that she had astonished him by her insight and swift understanding of him. He knew instinctively that she was right: he was indefinably different; he knew too that the difference in him was connected with his discovery of the white house and the Lomax family. Yet he had no wish to reveal this to Helen. It was a secret knowledge in his heart.

So he said at last: 'I cannot explain, Helen—not now, anyway.'

She nodded. 'Did you hear that Austen Bray is back in England?' she asked lightly, changing the subject. 'With a wife half his age and very attractive.' Desmond responded readily but while they talked Helen hid the ache in her being. With her sure instinct, she felt that his reluctance to discuss whatever it was that had changed him had to do with a woman. She had resigned herself to the knowledge that he would never marry her but she believed it was because Desmond was entirely self-sufficient and needed no partner through life. It was a different matter again if some woman had stirred him to emotion, achieving what she had been unable to accomplish during all the years that she had known and loved him.

He dropped Helen at her luxurious apartment before he returned to his office. With a promise to telephone her soon, he drove away with a wave of his hand. She stood on the pavement watching the car as it sped down the road. Her eyes were a little troubled.

She turned away and cannoned into a man who was hurrying along the pavement. He steadied her with a quick hand under her elbow. 'I'm so sorry,' she said. 'That was stupid of me.'

He smiled down at her. It was a nice smile— even, white teeth in a big, bronzed face. She had the swift impression of bigness and strength and outdoor vitality. He bent to pick up the books she had knocked from under his arm and she felt a stab of surprise for he did not seem the bookish type. 'Entirely my fault,' he assured her. 'I hope I didn't hurt you.'

She shook her head. 'Not at all.' She moved to leave him.

He seemed reluctant to let her go. 'That just proves the old saying—more haste, less speed,' he said lightly. 'I was trying to catch that bus.' He gestured towards a bus which had halted at traffic lights and was now drawing away, increasing its speed. He glanced at the watch on his wrist.

'I'm sorry,' she said again. 'It's so annoying to miss buses when you're in a hurry, isn't it?'

He shrugged easily and she noted again the

breadth of his massive shoulders. 'No point in hurrying now,' he said. 'I was fifteen minutes late for my appointment, anyway—I might as well skip it altogether.'

'Was it important?' she asked. It could have been politeness which kept her talking to him but she knew it to be the stirring of her old impetuosity.

He looked down at her and although she was tall she suddenly felt that he towered above her. 'It was for a job,' he said, 'but somehow I guess I'd have been unlucky. Firms don't usually take to a prospective employee who's late for an interview.' He grinned again. 'Don't worry about it,' he said easily. 'If I hadn't cannoned into you it would have been someone else—I wasn't meant to catch that bus, I know. I'm that kind of person, you see—always tearing about and never getting anywhere on time.'

Helen laughed. 'I hate punctual men,' she said but it had never been true before. Suddenly it was very true now.

He hesitated a moment then said, in a rush: 'Are you sure you're all right? There's a lot of weight behind me . . . look here, will you let me buy you a cup of coffee or something to make amends?'

She looked up at him, considering, then she nodded. 'I think that's an excellent idea.' He looked so pleased that she suddenly thought: 'Oh, but he's nice! Big and boisterous—and

42

terribly young—but nice!'

He looked about him and caught sight of a small restaurant. 'Shall we go over there?' he asked. They turned to the kerb and waited for the traffic to abate. Then he took her elbow with instinctive courtliness and they crossed the road. He ordered coffee once they were seated and then brought out a packet of cigarettes from his suit pocket. 'Do you smoke?' She accepted one and he fumbled for matches. She waited a few moments while he searched in vain then she opened her handbag and took out her slender, gold cigarette lighter with the diamond initials. She flicked it into life and offered it to him. He gestured quickly. 'Light your own first, please.' She did so and then he bent his head over the flame. She laid the lighter on the table for future use and looked up to find his eyes on it. 'That's an expensive trifle,' he said. Then he added quickly, a little awkwardly, 'It's very nice of you to have coffee with me.'

She raised an eyebrow. 'Why?'

He coloured a little. 'Well, I mean—a complete stranger . . .'

She laughed. 'We came into such violent contact that I don't think we can be considered strangers, do you?'

The coffee arrived in time to save him the reply. He toyed with the silver spoon. He turned his cigarette restlessly between the fingers of his other hand. She noted that he had nice, masculine hands which were well-kept but badly stained with nicotine. He followed her gaze. 'I smoke too much,' he said lightly. 'Force of habit.'

She wondered about him. How old he was, what kind of a job he had been hurrying after, why she had the strong impression that he was an outdoor type very much out of place in cosmopolitan London.

'Were you keen to get that job?' she asked slowly.

He did not look at her as he replied, 'Not so much on the work as the salary they offered.' Suddenly he glanced up and met her eyes. 'Beggars can't be choosers—not that I'm exactly a beggar but I might be reduced to that if I can't find a job.'

She wondered swiftly if he meant to touch her for money—there were devious ways that such men chose for this purpose. But she dismissed the idea immediately as ludicrous. She was sure that he was straightforward and direct as his way of speaking, as honest as his clear grey eyes and as friendly as his smile.

She picked up one of the books which lay on the table and studied its title. She grimaced a little at the heaviness of the subject. 'If you're familiar with this kind of thing, then you shouldn't find it difficult to get a job.'

He took the book from her and riffled through the pages. 'Unfortunately, I'm not familiar with it. I'm struggling to learn

44

something about it—but books were never in my line.' He grinned. 'As you can probably tell—I'm just not the studious type.'

'What is your type?' she asked.

He seemed a little taken aback. Then he said slowly, 'I've never really thought of myself as being any type—like everyone else, I like to think I'm really an individual!' His smile was quick to glow. 'At school I was always athletic—rowing, boxing, swimming, rugger— but I think it was more or less an outlet for me. I hated to be cooped up in classrooms—when I was out in the sun and the air I just crammed my time with energetic pursuits to stretch my cramped muscles and chase away all the dullness of learning from my reluctant brain.'

'And now?' she prompted.

'Now I hate to be cooped up anywhere,' he went on readily. 'Like this job I was going after—even if I'd landed it, I know damn well I wouldn't have stuck it very long. No office is big and airy enough for me—I hate desk work of any kind.'

'Then why go in for this line of business?' Once again she tapped the books.

'A chap I know told me there's money in it,' he replied frankly. 'But I doubt if the money's worth the frustration.'

'What would you really like to do?' she asked.

He drained his coffee. Then he stubbed his cigarette in the ashtray. Helen waited patiently for his answer. He looked down at his hands and flexed them slowly. She suddenly noticed their sensitivity. They were not hands for manual work despite his open-air outlook. They were the hands of a man who was capable of creation in some sphere—but she could not determine what sphere. He enlightened her immediately with his next words.

'I'll tell you,' he said with a rush of confidence. 'I want to live like a gipsy, wandering where I choose, putting to canvas all the beauty of *"this green and pleasant land"*.' She wondered in passing if he quoted consciously. 'I want to capture the life and the movement and the colour—I want to spend all my days, all my life, painting, painting, painting. I want to release the art in my soul and in my hands . . .' He broke off suddenly, embarrassed by the passion in his words. He looked at her and found her gaze to be sympathetic and understanding. Nevertheless, he said slowly, 'I don't know why I'm telling you all this. There isn't any reason why you should be interested.'

'Perhaps there isn't a reason but I'm still interested,' she assured him. 'Please go on.' He looked doubtful still. Helen leaned forward and pressed his hand with her slender fingers. Almost of their own volition, his fingers curved to clasp them.

'Of course I can't do this,' he said quietly. 'I

have to earn money to live—and I don't even know if my work is any good. I've been daubing on canvas since I was a kid but I've never had any expert opinion on my stuff. So I have to find a job. Then I'll scrape along on as little as I can and put aside the rest for the time when I can throw everything up and devote myself to painting.' He smiled a little shyly. He took his hand away and reached out for the packet of cigarettes. He offered them to Helen but she shook her head. He extracted one and stuck it between his lips. Helen flicked her lighter into life and held it towards him. This time he took the lighter from her and studied it before lighting his cigarette. Then he handed it back to her and rose to his feet. 'I guess I've taken up enough of your time,' he said and now there was a coldness between them. Helen felt that he had withdrawn into himself and she felt rebuffed. 'Thanks for listening,' he added. 'I'm afraid I get boring once I let my tongue run away with me.'

'I haven't been bored,' Helen said but because she was puzzled by his withdrawal her voice lacked the warmth of conviction. He looked down at her and his grey eyes were enigmatic. She rose to her feet and held out her hand. 'Thank you for the coffee.' He held her hand a brief moment. 'I hope you soon get a job,' she added.

He nodded. 'Thanks.' He walked with her out of the restaurant and they stood on the pavement together for a moment longer, but no words passed between them. He said abruptly, 'Do you live in those flats over the road?'

'Yes,' Helen said.

'Well—good-bye,' he said.

'Good-bye—and good luck.'

The strangely lopsided grin was back for a brief moment. 'Thanks—I'll need it.' Then he left her and hurried down the street away from her. She looked after his tall, powerful figure and wondered at the lithe grace of his movements for his size.

She let herself into her flat and threw her bag and gloves on to a table. Her thoughts were with the tall young man with the honest grey eyes, the forthright approach and the sensitive hands. Suddenly she paused as a thought came to her. She did not even know his name. She knew comparatively nothing about him. She would never see him again—and this last realization seemed to her to be completely wrong. It was important that they should meet again—if only so she could find out why he had suddenly rejected the feeling of companionship and warm confidence which had been between them in that small café with the dirty tablecloth and the thick, cracked cups.

Back at his office, Desmond Crane found himself unable to concentrate on the monologue which his colleague, Francis, was

48

delivering. However, Francis did not seem to notice his abstraction and Desmond knew from long experience that the man would continue unabated and indifferent to lack of reaction for many weary minutes yet. So Desmond sat back and let him talk . . .

The sense of quiet peace which filled the small white house: the rich quality in those two girls; his sudden realization that to walk alone through life was not a man's destiny—these were his thoughts. But they were threaded with a strange reluctance to return despite his longing to knock once more on the front door and feel the peace envelop him as he entered the house. He analysed the reluctance for what it was. At the moment, he had a treasure. If he returned, he might find that his memory deceived him—that it was not as he pictured it—that Isobel and Lisa Lomax were not as lovely, as good, as warm with loving kindness as he thought of them. There were no flaws and he had no wish to meet any. Was it not better to keep the memory sacred and never to risk disillusionment? Yet while he thought along these lines, he knew that he was compelled to return and he knew that it would be soon. He would risk disillusionment because he was confident that nothing would be changed.

He sought the intimacy of friendship with Isobel and Lisa Lomax: he sought the right to enter the house and know its welcome; he

49

wanted to offer friendship in all sincerity and in the depths of his heart he knew that at last it was possible for him to offer more to a woman—where before no woman had stirred him. But he must be patient. Friendship was a fine beginning: they had been kind and hospitable; he had furthered matters by sending flowers—coals to Newcastle, he told himself with a smile, thinking of the garden which was obviously tended with patience and loving care. Surely he would receive a note of thanks from them: it had been with this in mind that he enclosed his card. Soon he would present himself on the doorstep of the little white house—his excuse, he knew, a suitable gift for the boy as thanks for Michael's willing errand to the village.

He wondered about the reception they would give him. It provided fodder for his fertile imagination and his thoughts were far from the stout, perspiring Francis who prattled on unchecked.

He was possessed of a strange impatience with Francis, with his secretary, with the office and with the teeming life of London which surged about him—the heavy boom of the passing traffic was enough evidence of this. He felt a nostalgia for the country he had so recently left—the green fields, the proud trees and hedges bursting with new life, the azure, cloudless sky sailing leisurely over the countryside with the bright sun in all its majesty benevolently bestowing its warmth and light and colour . . .

With a slight sense of shock, he realized that Francis had ceased his monologue and was gazing at him inquiringly, a little puzzled and perhaps a little hurt at Desmond's apparent disinterest in his information. He pulled himself together and asked a question that was fortunately relevant to their interview.

CHAPTER FOUR

Lisa's slender hands expertly manoeuvred the wheelchair on to the path and then bowled it around the house.

Isobel had recently left for the village on a shopping trip and the sound of a car in the lane had stirred Lisa to action. She had been sitting in the garden behind the house, her sketch-book on her lap but her hands idle. A portable radio was playing quietly by her side and the song of the birds in the trees vied for her attention. But even the musical notes failed to draw her interest. She could not prevent her thoughts from wandering to Desmond Crane—she had, in fact, been sketching him from memory until her thoughts crowded out the memory of his tall handsomeness.

She wheeled her chair around the corner of

51

the house, fully expecting to find Frank Cummins at the gate. He frequently dropped off at the house on some pretext or other—but he was such an old friend, no pretext was necessary. He was always welcome and the two girls had a strong affection for him.

A low-slung sports car stood in the lane and walking up the garden path was the very man who had occupied her thoughts. She could not hide her astonishment at the sight of him.

Desmond crossed the lawn towards her and his smile was very warm. 'Hullo there!' he greeted her. 'I hope you don't mind this sudden descent—London is stifling in a heat wave so I ran away from it all.' He looked down at her, his eyes softening at the golden beauty of this woman and the joyous light in her eyes. 'You did say I might come again,' he reminded her.

'Of course we did—how nice to see you,' she said quickly. There was a hint of shyness in her next words. 'I wondered if we would ever see you again—people forget so easily.'

He gestured about him. 'I couldn't forget this place—or you and your sister.' His words were sincerely spoken and they brought a hint of colour to her cheeks.

She said, 'Shall we go to the back of the house?'

Immediately he moved instinctively to take the bar of the wheelchair. But with sudden sensitivity he stopped in his tracks. She placed her hands on the wheels and began to propel herself along the path. He walked beside her and felt his whole body relaxing, his mind absorbing the beauty and colour of the surroundings, his spirit soaking up the peaceful atmosphere.

She said suddenly, 'Thank you for not pushing me, Mr. Crane. I never like to feel that I'm completely helpless.' She went on quickly, 'Isobel walked to the village to do some shopping. She'll be back soon—I expect you'd like some tea to refresh you after your journey.'

'Where's Michael?' he asked. 'Has he gone with your sister? '

'No. He's probably over at the farm—our neighbour and good friend, Frank Cummins, farms near here and Michael loves to help him.' She smiled. 'He's a surprising blend of books and country life—the two don't always go together.'

Desmond replied slowly, 'They do in my case—I can only work in the country and feel that I've accomplished something satisfying. Any writing I do in Town always seems incomplete.' He added, 'But let me make the tea—I'm really quite capable at that sort of thing. If you tell me where everything is, I'll manage.'

At first she demurred but on his insistence she agreed to his suggestion. Within a very few minutes, he came out of the house with a tray which he laid on the table. He handed her a cup of the steaming, pleasant beverage and then drew up a chair beside her. He crossed one leg over the other and took out his cigarettes.

'This is very pleasant,' he said quietly. 'By the way, I brought a present for Michael—a model aeroplane. I hope he's interested in such things.'

'Very much,' she assured him. 'How kind you are!'

'Only in return for kindness,' he replied.

She shook her head. 'I can't believe that, Mr. Crane. I think you are a naturally kind person.'

'Desmond,' he corrected. He smiled disarmingly. 'That will be a kindness on your part. You see, I always think of you as Lisa— but if you are formal, then I must be too—and these surroundings just don't invite formality.' He noted again the rising of colour to her lovely face and his eyes twinkled. There was a momentary silence then he indicated her sketch-book. 'May I see some of your sketches?' She picked it up to hand it to him— then remembered that several leaves were covered with sketches of himself and she hesitated. Immediately he said, 'If you'd rather not . . .'

She placed the book in his hand. She was not ashamed for him to know that he had been the subject of her thoughts and sketches. Her

54

talent was undeniable and she knew that the sketches did him justice.

He looked through it with interest and they discussed one or two of the different sketches in the book. He was very much impressed and complimented her on her work.

Then he turned a leaf and found his own face looking up at him. It was cleverly done—a vivid portrayal—and he was touched by the faithfulness of her pencil. He said gently, 'You have a good memory, Lisa—I like this very much.'

She said instantly, 'Would you like to have it?'

'Yes, I would.' He turned over the leaf and this time he looked down at a sketch of Isobel and Michael. They were portrayed in the garden playing with bat and ball. Lisa had captured the eagerness of the boy and the laughing radiance of Isobel. He studied it for a long moment and he felt that the picture lived although it was only a black and white sketch. He closed the book slowly and handed it back to Lisa. 'You won't forget to let me have that sketch of myself,' he reminded her. He smiled. He was not surprised that she had spent some time on committing the memory of him to paper. It seemed perfectly natural that she should but this was not conceit on his part— just a natural acceptance of the easy intimacy which already existed between them.

They talked, then, for some time. Desmond

felt that he wanted to know as much about Lisa, her sister and young brother. He stored certain relevant facts carefully away in his mind. Lisa had thrown off the first hesitant shyness and talked easily to him of many things. Her sweet innocence attracted him. It was a rare thing indeed to talk with someone so completely unworldly yet who knew so much about life—not only from the books which gave her so much pleasure but from her acceptance of pain and sorrow, her approach to helplessness, and her pure simplicity of thought.

Isobel came down the lane, her shopping basket on her arm. The sun beat down on her uncovered fair head and she hummed softly to herself. Her fair skin had taken on a golden hue from the recent hot sunshine and the deep blue dress she wore emphasized her fair colouring.

She caught sight of the white sports car standing by the gate and the tune died on her lips. Her step faltered momentarily then she walked on again with purpose. So they had a visitor and she was in no doubt as to the identity of the car's owner. She had been thinking of Desmond Crane all day and while in the village she had known the strangest sensation—a tingling within her, an iciness in her veins and a lift of her heart. She had known then that he had come—as she had known he would before long. The flowers had been a warning of his return.

The couple on the stone terrace heard Isobel before they saw her. The click of the garden gate heralded her arrival in the stillness of the drowsy summer afternoon. Then the sound of her quick footsteps on the path as she came around the house. She turned the corner, saying lightly, 'I'm sorry I've been so long, Lisa.'

Desmond turned to look at her and she was just as he remembered—'of fair and shining beauty'. Her eyes met his and her gaze was calm and quiet. It did not disturb him that she showed no surprise at his presence. It was exactly as he hoped it would be. He rose to his feet and came towards her, relieving her of the shopping basket. They did not shake hands. As Desmond had already remarked to Lisa, the surroundings did not invite formality.

'Lisa hasn't been lonely,' he said with a twinkle in the depths of his blue eyes. 'How are you, Isobel?'

She barely noticed his use of her given name. She replied with her innate honesty: 'I knew you were here long before I saw your car. I'm glad you came back.'

'It would be very difficult to stay away,' he assured her. She smiled and glanced at Lisa. Then she turned to enter the house and he followed her, holding the heavy basket. Lisa watched them go in together and she knew then that something existed between them—a rare and precious something in which she had no part. It was as though a beam of light radiated from Desmond to Isobel. She opened her palms and found them criss-crossed with the marks of her finger nails.

Desmond placed the basket on the table and lounged against the door. He watched in silence as Isobel unpacked her purchases and put them away in cupboards. His presence did not seem to disturb her. She moved about the kitchen deftly and with swift grace and he watched her. He noted the rays of the sun catching the lights in her hair. He noted the sweetness of expression, the softly rounded bone formation of her face, the tender curve of her mouth.

'I had to come,' he said suddenly.

She did not look at him. 'I know.'

'This place—it calls to something inside me,' he tried to explain. 'It's like being away for many years—and suddenly coming home. Can you understand, Isobel?'

'Yes.'

The simple word was enough. He knew that she did understand what he was trying to say—he knew too that there was no need to put his feelings into words.

She turned to him and said with directness: 'You will always be welcome here, Desmond. We've waited for you a long time.' Her words were not strange to him. He nodded. She went on: 'Lisa and I need your friendship—there

58

are times when the loneliness here is too much—when I can do no more for Lisa because I am not enough. She needs someone like you.' A very sweet smile touched her lips. 'We are not very self-sufficient, you see.'

'Nor am I,' he admitted for the first time in his life. It was a great relief which brought him peace to feel the need of another human being whether through physical or spiritual contact. He lifted one of her hands and held it, looking down at the beautiful lines of the slim fingers, 'I wish I knew why you and Lisa are so kind to me,' he said slowly. 'A complete stranger who came into your life by accident—yet I feel that we've known each other all our lives.'

She looked up at him with her strangely pure gaze. 'You were never a stranger, Desmond. The moment you entered this house I knew that.'

He recalled with acute vividness that she had opened the door wide without hesitation and that the house had welcomed him without reservation as he entered. He remembered too that there had been no constraint between them, that she had accepted him naturally and without question. Now he understood why.

'Perhaps after all it was no accident that led me here,' he said quietly. 'Who are we to question the opportunities which life offers?'

'I never question anything,' she said.

And he knew that in this woman was the same acceptance of life that her sister shared.

59

He felt envy and admiration and a growing affection.

The day sped on wings. The boy, Michael, came home shortly before sunset. He greeted Desmond easily and without surprise. 'I've been looking over your car,' he said. 'Have you ever done eighty in her?'

Desmond grinned. 'Frequently—especially on my way here! Did you see that big package in the back?' Michael nodded. 'That's for you—you'd better go and get it, hadn't you?'

With a whoop of glee the boy ran off. He returned almost immediately, clutching the parcel. He paused a moment and looked at Desmond inquiringly. 'Is it really for me?' he asked.

'It is indeed. Open it up, Michael.'

The wrappings were torn off to reveal a model aeroplane. There was silence as Michael gazed at it with incredulity in his grey eyes. Then he put out a hand to touch it reverently. He turned to Desmond and gave him his hand. 'Thank you very much, sir,' he said quietly. 'It's the best present I've ever had.'

Desmond was touched and a little embarrassed by the boy's sincerity. He bent down and picked up the aeroplane. 'Let's go and see how it works,' he said lightly.

Isobel and Lisa watched the two with the aeroplane in the garden. Michael could barely

60

conceal his delight with the gift and Desmond was apparently as interested in its workings as the boy. Isobel turned to her sister with a smile. 'Now I know why people say there's something of the child in every man,' she said.

'You like him, don't you?' Lisa asked quietly.

'Very much.'

'So do I. I think he's a wonderful person—so kind and friendly. I think he likes being here, Isobel.'

'I know he does. I hope he comes often.' She glanced down at Lisa. 'He will be a good friend to us, Lisa.'

'Frank will be jealous,' her sister replied.

'That's nonsense! He has no reason to be jealous, after all. He will understand that Desmond is just a friend.' She looked again at the man and the boy as they stood, heads raised to the sky, watching the aeroplane in flight.

'Desmond needs us, Lisa. I can't understand it, or explain it, properly. But I know we can supply a need—perhaps it is just the peace and contentment here—or the friendship we can offer him—or else it is because he is lonely.'

'Lonely? But I expect he has lots of friends,' Lisa said quickly.

'He told me that coming here is like coming home,' Isobel said gently. 'I don't think he has any family of his own—so we must be like his family to him.'

A moment's silence then Lisa said with a catch in her voice: 'I don't think I could possibly accept him in the light of a brother, Isobel.'

Isobel brushed back a strand of the corn-coloured hair from her sister's brow. Bending down, she impulsively kissed the smooth white cheek. 'Don't weave dreams about him, darling—I know I said this to you before but I'm only trying to protect you. Desmond isn't seeking romance—only friendship. I don't want you to be hurt in any way—and if you get too fond of him, it will spoil things. He would stay away from us.'

Lisa's eyes were troubled. 'My foolish dreams won't hurt anyone, Isobel—and I can keep them to myself.'

'Keep in mind the fact that you've never known anyone like Desmond—and this might make you feel romantic about him. He's very attractive and very kind. It would be easy to love a man like him . . .' She broke off as he turned and hurried across the lawn towards them.

'That's a beautiful thing,' he said. 'She flies like a bird.'

Lisa laughed up at him. 'You're as thrilled as Michael with that ridiculous toy,' she mocked him.

'Second childhood, I expect,' he retorted. 'It's a long time since I played with model aeroplanes.'

'It was very good of you to give it to Michael,' Isobel said quietly.

'Purely selfish on my part,' he assured her. 'I love giving people presents—and I love giving them surprises, too.' He turned to watch Michael as he captured the returned aeroplane and prepared to send it soaring once more into the sky. 'He's a fine boy,' he said and there was a note of longing in his voice. He turned back to Isobel. 'I compliment you on his upbringing—it couldn't have been an easy matter. What were you—twelve or thirteen when your mother died?'

'Fourteen,' Lisa supplied. 'And I was eleven. Isobel took over everything wonderfully well.'

'I can believe that,' he replied with a quick smile for Isobel. 'She has a capable air.'

Isobel laughed. 'You're biased because you caught me in an apron, baking, the first time we met. You mistook me for Michael's mother!'

'I remember. I also remember that I thought you incredibly young for the part,' he returned. 'I'm curious to know where Michael inherited that mop of auburn hair.'

'From my father. He was auburn. My mother was fair—just like Lisa,' Isobel told him.

He looked down at Lisa. 'Yes. She is like her mother—and I'm speaking as one who has seen and admired "Portrait of Laura" which was your father's finest work.'

Lisa tilted her chin under his scrutiny. 'All of my father's paintings were fine,' she said proudly.

He nodded. 'I'll concede your point—but you must remember that I've seen very few of them. Most of his works were unsold, I believe.'

'There are several in the house,' Isobel told him. 'Would you like to see them?'

'I've studied the three in the sitting-room,' he told her. 'I noticed them last week. I should like to see the others.'

Isobel took him on a tour of the house. In almost every room hung her father's paintings. Above Lisa's bed, in the small room downstairs where she slept, hung a portrait of a mother and infant child. Desmond stood looking up at it and he was touched by the serenity of the woman's eyes and mouth, the rounded tenderness of the child's limbs. Isobel said: 'My mother and Lisa. My father painted it when Lisa was three months old. It's very good, don't you think?'

Desmond had always been interested in art and his knowledge was fairly widespread on the subject. His eyes glowed with appreciation. 'Excellent!' he approved. 'It glows with life. Your father was a brilliant artist. He should have sold more of his works, of course. There are so few of them on public exhibition.'

She shrugged. 'He occasionally made a

64

present of a painting to a favoured friend—but he kept most of them. He always said that it was not in him to create beauty for mercenary gain—it took away his enjoyment and his inspiration.' She smiled a little ruefully. 'I know exactly how he felt. I used to love scribbling my little stories. I started to write them for Michael when he was very young. Now, knowing that I have a contract with Hawtreys to fulfil, some of the sweetness has gone from my writing.'

He looked down at her. 'Think of the many children who know and love your little books, Isobel—it's so much more worthwhile to write for children than for cynical, worldly adults.' He sighed softly. 'A child wears the veil of illusion. I sometimes think it a great pity that it is torn away with ripening maturity.' He turned away from the painting and as he did so, his eye was caught and held by a miniature which stood by the bed. It was exquisite and delicate. A golden-haired child sitting on a lawn with her pale blue skirts billowing about her, laughing eyes and rosy, dimpled cheeks, small white teeth biting with apparent enjoyment a round, rosy apple which she held with both sweet, curving hands. Desmond caught his breath. 'How enchanting!' he exclaimed.

'Lisa again,' Isobel told him. 'I think that is my favourite among all my father's paintings.'

'It's incredibly vital,' Desmond said excitedly. Nigel Lomax had captured the crispness of the white apple with its rosy skin, even the trickle of juice from the child's lips which flowed down her small, rounded chin. This gave the miniature a touch of life. The delicate pastel shades of gold and blue and pink conveyed the innocence and enchantment of youth.

There were other paintings, all excellent and with the touch of genius which had been evident in those of Nigel Lomax's paintings he had seen before. But none held his interest so much as the miniature which stood on the small table by Lisa's bed. Once again, thinking of it as he sat in the cool evening quietude, listening vaguely to the murmur of conversation which passed between the sisters, he felt the same, strange pang which had assailed him at the sight of Michael on the lawn with the model aeroplane held high above his bright head. It was an ache he could not define. A sweet but painful yearning which the unconscious grace and youth of the boy's slight body and again the tenderness of the miniature had aroused in the depths of his soul.

Reluctantly, he took his farewell as the deep, comforting dusk descended and one or two stars came out in the sky above. He lifted a strand of Lisa's silken hair and smiled warmly down at her. 'I think you two girls have bewitched me,' he said lightly. 'I feel as though I never want to leave this enchanted castle.'

'Our spells are very potent,' Lisa returned with a gleam of amusement in her eyes. 'But stay, Desmond—we don't want you to go.' The invitation was impulsive.

He shook his head. 'Thank you—but it's impossible.' He bent down and brushed his lips against Lisa's cheek.

Isobel went with him to the door. 'I'll walk to the gate with you,' she offered.

He put his hand on her shoulder. 'No. Wait here and watch me go—I like to remember you that way.' He felt her slim body react to his touch. She trembled a little.

'When will you come again?' Her voice was low.

'Soon,' he promised. 'You will know, Isobel.'

She looked up at him. His eyes were very serious and in the pale lighting he looked suddenly very vulnerable. She smiled at him tremulously. 'Yes, I shall know.'

It was difficult to walk away from the shining purity of her gaze but he would not look back. He did not look back even when he drove the car away from the little white house. He knew exactly how she would look—how she would always look to him.

CHAPTER FIVE

It seemed that he had left a little of his personality behind. The house seemed to echo with his quiet, cultured voice. There was the memory of him in every room.

Isobel and Lisa talked little of him. But each had her private thoughts. Michael was the one who spoke of Desmond Crane.

'Why should he bring me the plane?' he demanded of Isobel as she busied herself in the kitchen. 'Why did he come back, anyway?'

'He came to see us because he appreciated our kindness,' she returned quietly. 'He's that kind of man. No little kindness would ever go unnoticed where Mr. Crane is concerned—that's why he brought you a present. It was kind of you to cycle into the village for Bert Stoner.'

'I had the best of the bargain,' he retorted in his strangely adult way of speaking, every word clear and precise. There were times when Isobel wondered if there were too little of the child in him—then she would hear his youthful shrieks of glee as he raced about the garden or think of his boyish distaste for soap and water and she would dismiss her thought of his precocity. 'I came back in the lorry. That was enough reward.'

She rumpled his hair. 'Mr. Crane likes to

give presents,' she told him. 'It was really far too expensive a gift—but I didn't have the heart to refuse it.'

'I'm jolly glad you didn't,' he said emphatically.

'None of the other boys at school have anything like it—and I won't swop it for anything!'

'You must never swop it,' she told him quickly. 'Mr. Crane would be very hurt.'

'I know,' he said slowly. 'Anyway, he's coming again soon and I'm going to take him up to Brierly Hill so we can fly the aeroplane from there. There should be a strong wind up there. I promised to take him through the woods, too, and show him the Hermit's Hideout and the pond. Do you think he'd be interested in The Folly, Isobel?'

She smiled. 'I think he'll be interested in any place where you take him, Michael.'

'Yes, that's what I thought,' he said solemnly. 'Hasn't he got any boys of his own, Isobel?'

'No,' she said. 'He isn't married. Why?'

'It's just that he seems to know quite a lot about boys—what they like, I mean, and the sort of things that interest them. Funny, we hardly know him at all and yet I feel that I've known him for ages.'

She was pleased that Michael had accepted him as readily as she had herself. But surely that was because her brother was a sensitive

69

little boy. It was odd and impossible to analyse this feeling that Desmond Crane belonged to them.

She found herself thinking about him, both consciously and otherwise. He invaded her thoughts both night and day. She could see his kind, sensitive and good-looking face very clearly. At times her shoulder tingled as though she felt again the touch of his hand. His voice rang in her ears and when this happened she felt the sudden startled lift of her heart.

One night she was drifting off to sleep, long lashes curved in crescents on her gently rounded cheeks, one hand cradling her face, the short fair hair rumpled by her pillows.

She heard her name spoken and then she had the strangest sensation that someone bent over her as she lay in bed. She opened her eyes quickly and her heart was racing, all her nerves tense with excitement. The room was empty and dark. She was completely alone, For a moment she wondered if Lisa had called her—then dismissed it. She knew that it had been Desmond's voice which spoke.

She lay on her back, her eyes wide open, trying to control the sudden violent trembling of her body, trying to persuade herself that it was purely a figment of her imagination, a result of his occupation of her thoughts. There was no other explanation. He was miles away and she had no reason to believe that she was in his thoughts. A tiny pulse throbbed heavily in her throat and she put up a hand to still it. How could she explain the sudden sense of his nearness to her, the echo of her name spoken by him—an echo which still lingered. She was suddenly very warm and she threw back the covers and slipped from her bed. Going to the window, she leaned out into the cool night air and let the breeze fan her hot cheeks. A few strands of her hair were caught and fluttered about her forehead by the night breeze. She looked up at the heavens. It was a particularly lovely night with the stars in all their glory, still and majestic in their appointed places. A velvety hush pervaded the air and from the garden below rose the sweet scent of the flowers she had planted with loving hands and tended so patiently.

She tried to marshal her thoughts into composure. There must be a logical explanation for her recent disturbing experience. But she could not find the logic. Her heart stirred again with the recollection. Was there some such affinity between Desmond and herself of which she had often heard and read but never before experienced? Did this explain their natural acceptance of each other, the lack of formal restraint between them, their mutual understanding, her recognisance of his need of their friendship and the peace which their home offered? She had not thought to analyse before. Even now she shrank from analysis because to her it was something rare and valuable—this feeling that she knew existed between them—a feeling which she had never defined but never denied.

Was it possible that his thoughts had been with her a few moments ago and this in some way explained why she felt his nearness and heard his voice? She knew that Desmond was a sensitive man and she responded with her own sensitivity.

But I am not in love with him, she told herself firmly. Whatever this is between us, it has no romantic basis. I feel that I know him so well—I feel that I've waited all my life to meet him and to know him—I feel that we think alike and feel alike—that we share something which is rare in this life—can I call it an affinity—or is that perhaps the wrong word? Is it possible for a man and a woman to have a deep—she paused in her thoughts—an affinity, a deep friendship . . .? Is it possible without the world attaching romantic strings to it—hinting and jesting and perhaps sneering? What of Lisa? Would she understand? She is half in love with Desmond now and I must not let her be hurt. If she misunderstood my feeling for him, she would be hurt. But how can I deny it? To deny what is between Desmond and I would be to deny myself—to lie to myself. But it isn't love—I swear it isn't love—I would know if I loved him . . . Lisa is so young, so lovely—she has so little and I have so much. I must not hurt her. If she does indeed love Desmond—then what do I do? He is kind and sensitive and good—but that doesn't mean that he will come to love Lisa. She could not bear his pity . . . but he would never offer that. He can understand her pride and sensitivity. He must see, though, that she's very fond of him already. Will that keep him away? Will he be afraid of hurting her? But how can he stay away—he knows that we need to be together occasionally, he and I—we need each other in some indefinable way. He is happy here—and I feel he has never had his share of happiness. He finds companionship here—and I feel he is a lonely man.

She remembered with sudden clarity the sense that he reminded them of his presence about the house. At least, she was reminded of him—she did not know how Lisa felt for she was very quiet and reluctant to speak of Desmond. Could it not be that he thought of them often and longed to be with them? There were stranger things in heaven and earth . . . she quoted unconsciously.

Her thoughts moved on. He is still with me, she told herself with realization. That is why I have this wonderful sense of well-being since he came. He walks with me and lives in my being. I can never be alone again. My life will never be the same again now that he has come into it . . . Nothing could sever the bond that flows between us . . .

At last she climbed back between cool sheets but sleep would not come to her for a very long time. She was at peace now that she had reached a conclusion. She understood now that in some inexplicable way his spirit had called to her across a long distance guided by his thoughts of her.

Desmond had sent a parcel of books to Lisa together with a letter. He had chosen the books with great care, remembering that they shared a preference for one particular author whose work was famous and much-loved. There was also a book of poems and on looking through, Lisa found a passage marked by him. She read it aloud and sudden tears pricked her eyelids. A few simple words, quietly-spoken, but they held a message.

'Never shall I leave again
My lady in her cloak
Of fair and shining beauty
When I return from wanderings abroad . . .'

Lisa sat very still, the open book in her hand. Hope had leaped in her heart as she read the lines of the poem. Time and again she had told herself that it was foolish to think too much about him but she could not help the joy in her heart. I love him, she exulted to herself now. I've loved him since the first time he smiled down at me. He's kind and good and understanding—he's sensitive, too, she told herself remembering his movement to push her wheelchair and then his instinctive forbearance. *'Of fair and shining beauty'*—if that is how he thinks of me then life has never been more wonderful. She read the passage again and her eyes were very warm, the curve of her lips sweet and tender. *' "Never shall I leave again" '* she quoted softly to herself. 'No, my darling—I'll never let you go. But how long will it be before you *"return from wanderings abroad"*? I am impatient for my love.'

Isobel came out of the house. She carried her workbasket and a shirt of Michael's lay across her arm. She sat down beside Lisa and placed the work-basket on the table.

'Another torn shirt,' she sighed. She glanced up from her inspection and observed Lisa's rapt face. 'Are you pleased with the books?' she asked gently.

'Isn't it thoughtful of him?' Lisa responded eagerly. 'He remembered that Purvis Kingsley is one of my favourite authors, too.' Suddenly, shyly, she held out the book of poems. 'Look, Isobel,' she said. 'He has marked this specially.'

Isobel took the book and read the marked passage. Her eyes were very thoughtful when she looked again at Lisa. 'It's beautiful,' she said slowly.

Lisa took the book back and hugged it against her youthful breast. 'It would be impossible to mistake his meaning,' she said happily. 'Oh, Isobel, I'm so happy—I'm sure he cares for me—and Isobel, I love him so much.'

Isobel had not expected this and her eyes were startled. 'Love him!' she exclaimed. She had known that her sister was weaving fanciful dreams in her heart but she had not known that Lisa had given that heart so readily to Desmond Crane.

Lisa nodded. 'Yes,' she said quietly. 'Please don't remind me that we know very little about him—that has nothing to do with it. I feel that I've known him all my life. I feel too that I've loved him all my life.' Her eyes were sparkling. With impulsive affection, she lifted the book of poems to her lips and kissed it. 'It was a lovely gesture to send me this,' she said. 'It's his way of telling me that he loves me too, I know.'

Isobel put aside the shirt and her expression was troubled. 'Don't leap to conclusions, darling,' she said slowly. 'It is possible that he marked that poem for another reason, you know—it could have been his own copy and perhaps he particularly likes that one poem. Please, Lisa—I'm so afraid you'll be hurt.' She paused for a moment, watching Lisa's face. She saw that her words had touched home for a trace of doubt had leaped to Lisa's eyes. 'I was afraid you were beginning to care for him,' she added gently. 'Be very sure that you mean what you've just said, darling. It's so easy to be mistaken. You're so young.'

Lisa shook her head stubbornly. 'I know how I feel,' she insisted. 'I do love him, Isobel. You've never been in love—you don't know what it's like, I won't listen to your misgivings. When you love someone as I love Desmond, then you'll know that he cares in return, I can't explain it—call it instinct, if you like.'

Isobel felt stunned. Lisa had never spoken to her so defiantly before. Without another word, she rose and went from the terrace into the garden. She walked to the bottom of the garden, trying to control the turmoil of her thoughts and feelings. Absently, she picked a few dead leaves from the flowers that grew there. There was dread in her heart for her beloved sister. She feared so much that Lisa was wrong. It was possible, of course, that Desmond had fallen in love with Lisa and that he had marked the poem deliberately so that she would understand this. But supposing her explanation had been the right one? Lisa would be hurt and bewildered—first love could be devastating and Isobel felt that Lisa would never love again. She was a single-minded person. She was impulsive, warm-hearted, and terribly innocent. When Desmond came again she would greet him like a lover—and if he felt only friendship and affection for her, then he would be puzzled and disturbed. He would be kind, Isobel knew, but honest—then he would go away and they

77

would never see him again. Her heart was filled with such pain at this thought that she lifted her head sharply—surely she was not in love with him herself? She had been convinced that love did not disturb the affinity she shared with him. But now doubt crept in. Why else should she dread his going away, out of her life, never to return again? Her whole body began to tremble . . .

Lisa called her name. She turned and slowly went back to the terrace, composing her expression, guarding her eyes so that Lisa should not read the realization which had shaken her so much.

'I'm sorry, Isobel,' Lisa said gently. 'I was rude to you.'

Isobel forced a smile to her lips. 'I didn't mean to be a wet blanket,' she said. 'I understand how you feel—you're possibly quite right.' Suddenly she knelt at her sister's feet and took her hands. 'Listen, darling— when he comes again, please don't rush your fences. If he does love you, then let him tell you so. Don't take it for granted on the strength of a few marked words in a poem. I'm so anxious for you, Lisa. I couldn't bear you to be hurt—I can't help thinking that you might be wrong.'

Lisa released one of her hands and stroked Isobel's hair. 'Don't worry,' she said. 'I won't do anything foolish—I'm not a child, Isobel.'

Isobel looked into her serene face, into the

suddenly wise eyes. 'No, you're not a child,' she repeated slowly. It seemed that Lisa had suddenly grown mature and now she could not doubt that her sister was in love. It shone from her eyes and gave her an aura of sweet contentment.

Frank noticed the change in her very quickly.

The very next day, as he drove Isobel to Hanleigh, he glanced sideways at her and said: 'What's happened to our Lisa? She seems a different person.'

'In what way?' Isobel was deliberately evasive.

Frank shrugged. He often found it difficult to put his thoughts and feelings into words. 'This may sound silly—but Lisa has always seemed outside our world. She's always been like someone standing on the threshold of the world we live in, a spectator in life. Now she's suddenly with us. She's radiant and excited about something. She used to be such a quiet, peaceful person. But now she acts as though she's bubbling over with some secret which she won't be able to keep to herself much longer.'

Isobel was silent, thinking of his words. Once again she was surprised by Frank. Despite the many years they had known each other and been friends, he still had the power to surprise with a sudden flash of insight. She realized the truth of what he had said. Lisa had always been a dreamer, inclined to wrap herself in a world of fantasy, keeping herself aloof and untouched from everyone in some indefinable way.

Before she could speak, Frank added with a light laugh: 'If it were anyone but Lisa, I'd have said that she's fallen in love with some man. But Lisa never meets any men—except me . . .' He broke off, startled, and glanced quickly at Isobel. 'You don't think . . .?'

Isobel shook her head. 'No. You're quite right, Frank—but I didn't realize you could be so discerning. Lisa is in love—with Desmond Crane.'

He creased his brow thoughtfully. Then he said, 'That chap who sent you the flowers and gave Michael his plane.'

'Yes. Do you remember, Frank? His car broke down and he came to us for help.'

'I remember. It's all very sudden, surely?'

Isobel shrugged slightly. 'Like a bolt from the blue,' she said. 'But that's how love is supposed to strike—according to all the books.'

He said tenderly: 'Poor Lisa.'

Isobel looked at him quickly. His eyes were on the winding ribbon of road before them, his strong, capable hands steady on the wheel.

'Why do you say that, Frank?'

'It must be pretty obvious. This man Crane—what do you know about him? He's a comparative stranger. He probably thinks of you and Lisa as kind people who helped him

80

out once—and he's grateful. I don't suppose he's given Lisa a thought as a woman. Even if he was attracted to her, it isn't likely that he'd pursue it any further—a girl like Lisa—I mean, well, Isobel, she is a cripple and no healthy man saddles himself with a paralysed wife. What kind of marriage would it be?'

Isobel's hands were firmly clasped together in anguish. This was one line of thought which had not occurred to her. Now she realized the truth of it. Of course, Frank was right. Desmond was unlikely to let himself fall in love with a girl like Lisa—and if he had, he would never offer marriage. The conditions of such a marriage would be impossible. Lisa herself must realize this. They could not hope for any happiness together. Lisa was so used to her own helplessness that she no longer thought of its effect on anyone else.

'Hasn't Lisa thought of it like that?' Frank asked anxiously.

'I doubt it very much,' Isobel replied unsteadily. 'She is convinced that Desmond loves her. To Lisa, love conquers all. I expect she thinks that if they love each other, then there is nothing to prevent marriage between them. She is so innocent, Frank—you can't imagine how much so. She wouldn't see any flaws in a man like Desmond marrying a cripple. If I tackle her on it, she's sure to say that their love will be enough—that it's a pity they can't have children but they can be happy without them—that Desmond wouldn't expect a wife who can run his home and do all the things that I do because he's wealthy enough to afford servants to take care of that. I know Lisa so well. She's living on a cloud at the moment. She thinks only of her love for him and the way he feels about her.'

'Has he said anything to her? Has he written to her?' Frank wanted to know.

Isobel explained quickly the circumstance of the book of verses and the marked passage. Frank pursed his lips thoughtfully as they drove into the High Street of Hanleigh.

'She's banking a lot on something that might not mean a thing,' he commented. 'I know what I would do.' Isobel looked at him with inquiry in her lovely eyes. 'Yes, I know what I'd do,' he repeated. 'Write to Crane and explain that Lisa is feeling romantic about him—tell him not to come any more for her sake—and then hope that in time Lisa will forget all about him.'

'I couldn't do that!' she exclaimed involuntarily. The very thought that she might never see Desmond again struck at her heart—and this time she admitted sadly to herself that she did love him. He had caused more turmoil by his unexpected entry into their lives than she had ever imagined could happen.

Frank turned his head to look at her. There had been a note in her voice which struck him forcibly and he told himself that Lisa was not the only one who was feeling romantic about this stranger. He felt a spurt of resentment but he said nothing as he pulled the car to a stop and turned off the ignition. There was nothing to say.

CHAPTER SIX

The big, powerfully-built young man strode through the crowds that thronged the pavement. Several turned to look at him for his deep tan and burly height drew attention.

Helen Fairfax suddenly leaned forward on the cool leather seat of her taxi. She tapped on the glass pane and drew it back to speak to the cabby.

'Pull up here, will you. I've changed my mind.'

Hastily she stepped out, thrust some silver into the resigned cabby's hand, and swiftly hastened after the young man. He walked without looking either left or right until he reached a side street. Then he paused at the kerb, waiting impatiently for the traffic to lessen. Helen caught up with him and touched his arm. He turned, a little startled but at sight of her a broad grin spread across his pleasant face.

'Hallo there!' he exclaimed.

'Are you always in such a hurry?' she

83

laughed up at him. 'On your way to another interview?'

He grinned. 'Not this time. I'm just walking off a bad temper. How nice to see you again!'

'I hope you mean that,' she said lightly. 'The last time we met you rushed off as though you regretted ever bumping into me!'

Dull colour stained his face, deepening the tan. 'I did leave you rather abruptly,' he admitted.

She said quickly, 'Well, now we've met again accidentally, won't you let me return the compliment—have you time to have coffee with me?'

He hesitated perceptibly for a moment. Then he smiled down at her. 'That would be very nice—thank you.'

They were jostled as impatient pedestrians surged across the road now that the traffic lights had changed. She caught his arm. 'We'd better move on,' she said, 'Look—if you really aren't going anywhere, why not come up to my flat to have coffee. It's more peaceful than a public place, It's only a few minutes walk from here.'

Again that momentary pause. Then he nodded and they walked on.

'How are you getting on?' she asked him impulsively. 'Did you land a job yet?'

'I did—but I chucked it yesterday after rowing with my immediate superior.' His grin was a little sheepish. 'I told you that I felt too cramped in an office.'

Helen's first astonishment at seeing him had faded. It had worried her a little that she might never see him again for she had liked this tall, earnest young man with his love for art and his dislike of conventionality.

She laughed. 'I think you'd better start out on your gipsy life as soon as possible—you're so obviously not cut out for city life.' She thought in passing that he was a striking figure in the midst of this bustle and dirt and noise. Despite his rather mediocre colouring, he had personality—vivid and impressive. She went on, 'I was on my way to have tea with a friend but I'm going to cut the appointment. I want to hear all about your short-lived job!'

His eyes were a little puzzled as he glanced at her. Admiration immediately took the place of bewilderment for she was looking very lovely. The raven hair was piled high at the back of her head and the deep blue eyes looked up at him with warm pleasure in their expression. Her tailored suit was the exact colouring of her eyes and fitted her slim figure to perfection.

They spoke of generalities until they reached the big block where she lived. As they walked across the foyer to the lift, he said, 'I can't get over meeting you again like that—London's such a big place.'

She flashed him one of her lovely, warm smiles. 'It can be a very small place, too, my dear—I couldn't believe my eyes when I saw you striding through the crowds. I was in a passing taxi so I paid it off immediately and came after you. I've thought about you several times since the day we met.' She felt no embarrassment at this confession.

It was his turn to confess. 'I've toyed with the idea of hanging around outside these flats in the hope of seeing you again. It would have been very presumptuous of me—but you seemed so interested in all I told you about myself. At least, you said you weren't bored.'

'And I wasn't,' she assured him. 'But, you see—it wasn't necessary for you to contrive a meeting. Fate stepped in again!'

Her flat was on the fourth floor and they stepped into the lift. 'You're soon back, Miss Fairfax,' commented the attendant as he closed the lift doors. Within seconds, they were stepping out on to thick, luxurious carpeting and walking along the corridor to her apartment door.

He said suddenly, 'Well, now I know your name, anyway. I realized that I never introduced myself before. I'm Ryan Nesbit.'

'Ryan?' Helen repeated. 'How unusual—and rather nice.'

They entered the flat and she threw her gloves and handbag on to a low table in the lounge. He stood looking around the room with its expensive décor and furnishings. His eyes were enigmatic and she glanced at him, puzzled. 'Come and sit down,' she invited. She crossed to the wall and pressed the bell-push. He sat down on a comfortable settee and crossed one leg over the other. She went back to him and picked up a cedarwood box from a coffee-table beside the settee. She opened it and offered him a cigarette.

'You've a lovely place,' he approved.

She smiled. 'Thank you. It is very nice.' A maid came into the room and Helen turned to her, 'Oh, Lucille, coffee please—I changed my mind about having tea out.' As the maid withdrew, Helen picked up a telephone receiver. 'Excuse me, Ryan—I must ring my friend now or she'll think I've been run over or kidnapped or something equally dire.'

He rose and went over to the long glass windows as she spoke in low tones over the telephone. He looked down on the busy street below, teeming with traffic and hurrying people. Strangely, much as he had thought about this beautiful, friendly woman and wanted to see her again, now he regretted their second accidental meeting and his acceptance of her offer of coffee. It struck him forcibly that she was a wealthy woman and it was presumptive of him to continue any association with her. But he had been unable to banish her from his thoughts and he believed that she was really interested in him. She had certainly seemed delighted to see him again—and there had been no need for her to pay off her taxi and hasten after him down the busy thoroughfare. An interest motivated purely by friendship, of course—he was willing to accept this. He wondered at her reaction when he told her that he had toyed with the idea of hanging about in the hope of seeing her. It was true that the impulse had moved him. Not knowing her name, yet wishing to see her again, it had seemed the only way. For the past week, he had passed the block of luxury flats again and again, scanning the entrance in the hope that she might come out or enter. Today, without any effort on his part, they had met. He smiled to himself slightly. He must have sounded like a young boy in the first throes of calf-love—he was glad that he hadn't admitted the many times he had passed the flats, hoping anxiously for a sight of her.

Helen replaced the receiver. She went over to join him by the window. 'I'm absolutely in disgrace with Nora,' she said lightly, 'but time will put that right. You know, I'm so pleased that we met again,' she said frankly for the second time.

He looked down at her and once again she felt that he towered above her. She liked the feeling. 'You really mean that, don't you?' he asked oddly. It was not so much a question as a statement.

Helen nodded. 'Yes. Life plays some strange tricks at times. Usually, one bumps into someone in the street—an apology is made by both—then each continues on their way without another thought. Ships that pass in the night,' she added with a little laugh. 'Sometimes, I think that's rather sad, though. Supposing a man bumps into a girl and feels an immediate attraction? Oh, it does happen,' she added quickly. 'Perhaps rarely, but it does happen. She walks in and out of his life in a split second and for the rest of his life he searches for her in vain.' She broke off and looked up at him eagerly. 'Do I sound terribly romantic?'

'Not at all. I know exactly what you mean—I suppose it could happen around the other way, too. I mean, the girl could be attracted to the man...'

A light came into her eyes and she was glad that Lucille returned at that moment. She thanked the maid and dismissed her, then busied herself with the delicate silver and china ware. 'Do you prefer your coffee black or white?' she asked,

'White,' he returned. She handed him the cup. 'Thank you.' He noticed that her own coffee was black and unsweetened. He said slowly, 'I think it would have been a great pity if we had passed on without another word.'

She looked at him quickly, searching his eyes. She read sincerity in their depths and her heart lifted a little. She reached for the cigarette-box to cover the sweet confusion which swept through her but in an instant he produced a packet from his jacket pocket and offered them.

'Have one of mine.' She accepted and he brought out his lighter, well-worn, very masculine but highly efficient. When both cigarettes were alight, there was a silence between them. Helen stirred her coffee idly. He sat back and watched the drift of blue-grey cigarette smoke in the draught from the open window. 'I talked so much the last time we met,' he said abruptly. 'Now, I can't think of anything to say, Miss Fairfax.'

'Please—Helen is my first name,' she told him swiftly.

He studied her and a trace of a smile touched his lips. 'Appropriate,' he commented. 'The face that launched a thousand ships—and broke a thousand hearts!'

She laughed. 'Helen of Troy? I think the resemblance ends with the name!'

'I don't agree,' he said. 'I've always understood that she was a very beautiful woman—so are you.'

The compliment was unexpected and she was taken aback for a few seconds. Then she said quietly, 'Thank you, Ryan.' She added quickly, 'Tell me how you were given such an unusual name.'

He shrugged slightly. 'My mother was Irish—it was her maiden name. An odd practice, I think.' He smiled at her. 'However, I'm more fortunate than my brothers who are blessed with Damon and Carey.'

Helen considered the man by her side. He seemed a little more at his ease now. She thought again how young he was—almost naïve at times. But perhaps it was merely his impulsive, direct approach. She liked the crispness of his mid-brown hair and the frankness of his grey eyes. She liked the big, pleasant face with its healthy tan. She liked the powerful physique of his big body in the rather shabby suit. 'What are you going to do now?' she asked him. 'Look around for another job?'

'I should,' he said, 'but I'm very reluctant. I feel the creative urge—I want all my time for painting. Unfortunately, I also want to eat—and smoke,' he added ruefully, studying his nicotine-stained fingers.

'Where are you living?' she asked. 'Do you have any facilities for working?'

'I'm renting a room in South London,' he told her. 'It's impossible to paint there—the atmosphere is entirely wrong—too much noise. My landlady has four small children and a variety of neighbours who pop in at all times of the day to drink tea and gossip. They eye me rather suspiciously whenever I go out or come in—I've a feeling that my landlady is anxious about her rent now that I've thrown up my job. I can afford to pay her two more weeks—so I must either find myself another job very quickly or take to the roads like a gipsy. I don't know why I'm telling you all this,' he said abruptly. 'We're from different worlds and I've no right to intrude in your life—or bore you with my financial difficulties.'

Helen laid her hand quickly on his arm. 'I wish you wouldn't say such things, Ryan. It isn't an intrusion—I'm honestly glad to see you again. I like being with you. I like talking to you. I'd like—in some way—to help you.'

She realized that she had said the wrong thing. He put down his cup of coffee and stood up. 'I must be going. It was nice of you to come after me, Miss Fairfax—but I should have made some polite excuse not to have coffee with you. I assure you that it wasn't for any mercenary reason that I accepted your invitation.'

Helen's eyes were reproachful. 'Please—sit down again. I've no intention of offering you money—give me credit for some understanding. Of course you didn't come for mercenary reasons—the thought never occurred to me. Do sit down, Ryan, and have some more coffee.'

'I'd rather not, thanks, I do appreciate your kindness—I hate to be blunt, but it would be very foolish for us to form any kind of friendship. As I said, we come from different worlds . . .'

'Ryan.' She spoke gently and he looked down at her with swift bewilderment in his eyes. 'I'd like to be your friend. I like you very much—and if you walk out on me now, I shall be extremely hurt. We would probably never meet again—Fate isn't that kind. Don't shut me out of your life now that we have met—these things all have a reason behind them, you know.'

'You're a strange woman,' he said slowly. He ran a hand through his springy, mid-brown hair.

She smiled. 'You're a strange man—we should be able to understand each other.'

For a long moment he looked into her eyes. Then Ryan took her hands and drew her slowly to her feet. He bent his head and touched her lips very gently, almost reverently, with his own. Her arms went up about his neck, drawing him closer, and suddenly he caught her to him and held her against his thudding heart. He kissed her again and there was warmth and the hint of passion behind the embrace they shared. When their lips parted, he still held her close, his cheek against the raven hair, his hands moving gently on her back, caressing. Helen was besieged by a strange, sweet emotion which caught at her blood.

She lifted her head and smiled up at him. 'This is crazy,' she said richly. 'But wonderful!' She realized now that she had wanted his arms about her, his lips on hers, the intimacy of his embrace, since their first meeting. He stirred her being with emotion she had never before experienced. Wild, impulsive longing held her captive.

He brushed her lips again with his mouth, then he released her. 'It is crazy,' he said, turning away from her. Trembling with the passion she had aroused, he did not dare to hold her any longer. 'I should never have kissed you, Helen—I haven't any right to make love to you.' He swung on his heel. 'I don't even know if you're married or engaged—or anything.' He laughed wryly. 'Come to that, I don't know anything about you!'

'Does that matter?' she asked. 'I wanted you to kiss me.' She smiled across the room at him.

He came back to her and took her hands. His eyes were very serious. 'You mean you're in love with me?'

Helen hesitated. Love. She had loved Desmond for years. This present emotion bore no relationship to the feeling she had always known for Desmond.

He noticed the hesitation and he said quickly, 'I'm sorry. That was a ridiculous question—forget I ever asked it, will you?'

She hardly heard what he said for the tumult in her being. The touch of his hands had awoken another surge of the heady rapture but she needed time to analyse her feelings. Perhaps this was love. Perhaps she had never loved Desmond—merely mistaken friendly, warm affection for the much stronger emotion. Common sense told her to go slow, to take time, to be very sure before she spoke of love to this man. She was twenty-eight and she could not afford to make mistakes. Twenty-eight years old and she had never wanted marriage, not even with Desmond for she had long since accepted that he was not the kind of man one could tie down with domestic strings. She had been content to love him—but if it had been love she felt for Desmond, would she have been so content? Did not love of itself bring in its wake impatience and the urge to marry and create a home and family atmosphere to foster that love?

Since Ryan Nesbit had come into her life, she had known a vague restlessness, a dissatisfaction, a longing for something she could not define. Astonished, she realized now that she had known too a new maturity—a sudden feeling that she had left the past behind her and that the future was opening up before her, promising new happiness and a new life. Now she connected the two happenings—but still she hesitated to call the bond between them 'love'. That there was a bond she readily admitted. It had seemed vital that they should meet again and she had been grieved that she knew so little of him, thinking of him as impossible to trace in a vast city like London. Never once had she thought that he might not want to meet her again. In her heart, she had known that he too sensed the bond between them—and in her heart, too, she had known his reasons for leaving her so abruptly before, remembering her wealth, her life, her wide circle of friends and realizing that he was a proud man who might think that these things would make a difference.

'Helen.' He spoke her name quietly and she came out of her reverie. 'Do you want me to go now?' he asked.

She shook her head. 'No.' She released her hands and sat down slowly. 'Let's have fresh coffee,' she suggested. 'You haven't told me anything about that job of yours,' she went on easily. 'I want to know what style of painting you specialize in, too. There are so many things to talk about, my dear—so many things I want to know about you.'

A slow smile touched his lips. 'I'm afraid talking got a little side-tracked by action,' he said and she liked the hint of laugher in his voice. It eased the atmosphere immediately. She patted the cushioned settee by her side and he sat down. 'Am I forgiven?' he asked gently.

She smiled at him readily. 'There's nothing to forgive, Ryan.'

She poured fresh coffee and he talked then; he spoke easily and with enthusiasm about his work—passed lightly over the subject of his office job and the circumstances which had led up to his leaving with the abruptness which was typical of him; amused her with an account of his life in the South London digs where his landlady thought him 'odd' and the children were attracted by his pleasant charm and gladly modelled for him at his request; touched her by his obvious longing to break away from the city life and go somewhere peaceful and lovely to paint to his heart's content.

At last, he took his farewell. They were both reluctant to part but Helen had to dress for a dinner party and he told her that he had an appointment to meet an old school friend for a drink that evening. Time had slipped by on wings. He had found it very easy to talk to her and she had found it very easy to listen. They had drawn very close during that time yet not once had their hands touched while they sat together on the settee and when he left he made no attempt to kiss her again.

'Will I see you again?' she asked eagerly.

He looked down at her. 'Is it wise, Helen?'

Disappointment flooded her and it was tinged with a sense of humiliation that she should have advanced so eagerly towards the rebuff.

'Of course, if you'd rather not, I shall understand,' she said swiftly, a little coolly.

He was very patient and very tender as he lifted a strand of hair from her brow and smoothed it back into place. The gesture made her feel suddenly very humble and rather ashamed of her quick words and offended feelings. 'I'm thinking of you,' he told her gently. 'I want to see you again . . . but I can't forget that you live in one world and I live in another, I shall never forget it. If you're going to be hurt in any way at a later date, then it's better if we say good-bye now and never meet again.'

The fact of his pride smote her deeply. She could not mistake his meaning and pain engulfed her for the moment. Then she said, 'I'll take the risk, Ryan.'

There was a silence. Then he nodded, 'I'll call you,' he promised.

It was unsatisfactory but Helen had to accept it. When he had gone, with a quick smile and a word of thanks for the coffee, she helped herself to a cigarette and curled up on the settee, not caring for the immaculacy of her elegant, tailored suit. She was thoughtful, the smoke wreathing up about her lovely head. He had gone without saying good-bye and she was glad of this. The word held a note of finality and surely this was only the beginning. But where would a friendship between them lead? If she was indeed in love with him would his pride allow him to accept it with ease? Was she wrong in thinking that the warmth in her heart found a response in him? At this thought she felt a sadness steal over her. But if their friendship developed into a mutual love would this mean marriage between them—or would that evil pride prevent it? For the first time in her life she really regretted the money which had always surrounded her and provided her with all she could ever want.

CHAPTER SEVEN

Desmond strode down the already familiar garden path to the front door of the little white house. Before he could raise the knocker, however, the door was opened to him by Isobel. He smiled down at her. Once more he had arrived without warning but the warm light in Isobel's eyes and the note of pleasure in her voice as she greeted him absolved him from any guilt he might have felt at his unexpected descent on them.

'I saw the car,' Isobel explained, as she closed the door behind him. 'I had a feeling you would come today.'

He placed a casual hand on her shoulder as they turned to enter the sitting-room. 'Telepathy,' he said lightly.

She smiled up at him but she was feeling a momentary apprehension. How would Lisa greet him? Her sister had assured her that she was not likely to do anything foolish when Desmond Crane came again—but if she were surprised by his arrival then she might show her feelings in the first moments of seeing him. Before they entered the sitting-room where Lisa was helping Michael with a jigsaw puzzle,

99

should she have a few private words with Desmond and explain the situation? Would he understand and explain that he had purposely come to see Lisa because he cared for her in return? Or would he be taken aback and a little anxious about the effect of his visit on Lisa?

She turned to him, the words on her lips but then her courage failed her and she merely said, 'Lisa will be pleased to see you. She was delighted with the books you sent.'

Lisa looked up from the table where the puzzle was laid out, nearing completion. Her heart lifted as she saw Desmond but she guarded her expression. She had thought often of Isobel's words and she could not deny a vague fear that her sister's explanation of the marked passage had been the right one. She would be patient—if Desmond loved her, she would know in time.

Michael welcomed Desmond before Lisa could speak. 'We won't be able to fly our plane from Brierly Hill in this weather,' he said as casually as though Desmond had never been away.

Desmond grinned at him. 'It still works then?'

'Of course! I'm taking great care of it ...'

'It must be the first thing Michael has ever had that hasn't been to pieces within a few hours,' Isobel put in.

Desmond crossed over to the table and

100

looked down at the puzzle. 'Surprised to see me again so soon, Lisa?' he asked lightly, absently picking up a piece of the jigsaw and inserting it in its place.

'Surprised—but very pleased,' she returned.

He turned his head to smile at her. 'I can't keep away for long,' he confessed. 'This place holds an irresistible attraction for me—you're sure I'm not a nuisance?'

Lisa threw him a reproachful glance. 'You could never be that, Desmond.'

He drew up a chair. 'Seems like I've arrived in time to help you finish this puzzle.'

'We've been trying to do it for hours!' Michael exaggerated, his auburn head bent over the pieces, his young brow creased by a puzzled frown.

Isobel slipped out to the kitchen. There was plenty to do and she knew that the jigsaw would keep them occupied for some little while. Frank had brought it for Michael on the previous evening—another of the little gifts that he never failed to bring with him.

As she beat the mixture for some small cakes, she could hear their voices mingling with merry laughter and she knew relief. As usual, Desmond had slipped into the easy familiarity of the house and fortunately Lisa had not given away the depth of her emotions. She had been a little surprised by Lisa's natural acceptance of his presence. Surprised but grateful that there had been no awkward

101

moment or embarrassment. Michael, who was often shy with strangers, seemed perfectly at his ease with Desmond too—but the man had great charm and an ease of manner which imparted itself to others.

She had been truthful when she told Desmond that she had known he would come. She had woken that morning with a quiet joy in her heart and her first thoughts had been of him. All morning she had been aware of a feeling of expectancy. While Lisa and Michael were concentrating on the jigsaw, she had been standing at the window, watching the rain and longing for the dark clouds to pass. But even the bad weather had been unable to cast a depression.

Even before she saw the car coming down the lane towards the house, she had known Desmond was in the vicinity by the wild beating of her heart and the curious sensation in her veins. A sweet smile had curved her lips as he stepped from the car and pushed open the gate. As he took the first purposeful strides along the path, she had turned to look at her sister. Lisa had looked up with a question in her eyes at the sound of the car. Their eyes met.

'Desmond?' Lisa had breathed his name.

'Be careful, darling.'

Lisa accepted the warning. 'Don't worry, Isobel.'

Then she had hurried from the room to

102

open the front door to the man who had caused such a furore in their quiet lives. Her heart had been thudding painfully and her welcoming words were a little tremulous for as she looked up into his handsome face and met the brilliant blue of his eyes she had been fully convinced that she loved this man. There had been little doubt before but now there was none.

As she slipped the batch of cake mixture into the warm oven, she came to terms with herself. She might love Desmond but he would never know her feelings. If it were meant that he should love Lisa and want to marry her, then there should be no outcry from Isobel. She would be glad to scc hcr sister's happiness and would give her blessing in all sincerity. If there were any way in which she could further Lisa's interests she would take it. But if there were any sign that Lisa was going to be hurt by Desmond Crane, then she would take steps to prevent it—even if it meant breaking their friendship with him and never again knowing the joy of his presence in their home.

Later that day, Desmond mentioned casually that he hoped the village pub would be able to put him up for the night. Instantly Lisa turned to her sister. 'But he can stay here, can't he? You don't mind, do you, Isobel?'

Desmond protested. 'No, I couldn't do that. I shall find somewhere to stay. Hanleigh isn't far even if the village pub can't oblige.'

Michael put in quickly, 'You can have my room if you like. I can sleep on the sofa in here—I'd like that!'

Desmond waited for Isobel to speak. She leaned forward to put another log on the fire she had lit because of the damp atmosphere. Outside, the rain was relentless in its beating on the windows. The fire gave the big room a cosy, welcoming appearance. The firelight reflected on her lovely face and he sought her expression eagerly. Was there a hint of reluctance in her silence?

At last she said, 'Of course you can stay. I wouldn't send you out in this weather to scour the countryside for a bed, Desmond.'

'I'll gladly sleep on the sofa,' he said. 'I don't want to turn Michael out of his bed.'

She smiled at that. 'Don't disappoint him—it's always a novelty for him to sleep on the sofa.'

So it was agreed. The evening seemed to pass very quickly. They talked easily together and were at times silent with the companionship of easy silence. Dusk fell and the rain ceased its steady patter. A few minutes later, a knock came on the front door and when Isobel answered it, she found Frank standing there. She closed the door behind him and he said, 'You've visitors? I saw the car outside.'

'It's only Desmond,' she said quickly. 'Desmond Crane. I'm glad you've come,

104

Frank—I wanted you to meet him.'

He nodded but a spasm of jealousy caught him at that moment. He followed her into the sitting-room and at sight of him, Desmond rose to his feet. Isobel made the introduction and the two men shook hands. Frank was unusually curt for him. He turned to Michael. 'You're up late tonight, lad,' he said.

'I'm sleeping on the sofa tonight,' Michael replied. 'Desmond is having my room. Do you think it will be raining tomorrow, Frank? We want to go up to Brierly Hill to fly my plane.' He went directly to the subject nearest his heart at the moment.

Frank shook his head. 'The rain's settled for a few days, Michael—we need it, you know, after all the hot weather.' He sat down in his usual armchair and brought out his pipe. Glancing at Desmond, who had relaxed again on the comfortable settee and was lounging comfortably, very much at home, he said: 'Good looking car you've got—makes my little Ford look very shabby. But she's a faithful friend and I wouldn't trade her.' He added abruptly, 'I should have thought a city chap like you would have kept away from the country when its wet. There isn't much doing in these parts when it rains, you know.'

Desmond sensed the hostility in the farmer's tone and was puzzled by it. However, he replied easily enough: 'Oh, I like the country in all weathers. I'm not a "city chap" from choice—only because of my business.'

'What is your business?' Frank asked.

Lisa replied quickly: 'I've already told you that, Frank—Desmond is a publisher.'

'I'm primarily a writer when business allows,' Desmond put in smoothly. 'But I understand that you're a farmer so I doubt if you have much time for books. It's a busy life, isn't it?' He had touched on the right subject and for the next few minutes Frank talked of farming and country life. The two women listened without interruption but Michael occasionally interposed a remark which he thought would enlighten Desmond on an obscure point of farming. He was very knowledgeable on the subject for his tender years.

Isobel knew instinctively that the two men did not like each other. She had wanted Frank to like Desmond and she was aware of a vague sense of hurt that he had disappointed her. She exchanged a glance with her sister and because their thoughts were so attuned she knew that Lisa too was disappointed at the turn of events. Frank was a very good friend to them of long standing and Isobel wondered if his hostility was born of jealousy that their friendship with Desmond Crane had taken such strides in a short time. He was a simple, straightforward man and he would not appreciate the finer points of their association with Desmond—the harmony of spirit, the mental affinity, the attunement of senses.

Frank left them much sooner than was his wont and Isobel went to the door with him. He looked down at her with serious eyes. 'Did you know he was coming?' he asked a little resentfully.

'No,' she replied honestly. 'But we were delighted to see him. We're all very fond of him, Frank.'

'Why does he keep coming here? I shouldn't have said there was anything to hold his interest—he must have plenty of friends and plenty of entertainment in London without seeking it elsewhere.'

'Perhaps we provide something he doesn't find in his other friends—or in other kinds of entertainment,' she said slowly. 'I think he needs us, Frank—I can't explain why. But as long as we can give him whatever it is that he needs, then he is welcome here. I'm sorry that you don't like him—I hoped you would.'

He grinned a little ruefully. 'I hope I didn't make it too obvious,' he said. 'I admit I don't like him—but I've no wish to offend the chap.' He opened the front door and looked up at the sky. 'I suppose you'll be too busy to go over to Weatherings tomorrow now?'

Isobel caught his arm. 'Oh, Frank—I'd forgotten! I'm sorry—but I shall be too busy. I can't leave them to fend for themselves. Not now, anyway. Michael would have looked after Lisa for me—but I can't expect him to cope with Desmond, too. I'm sorry, Frank,' she repeated slowly.

He shrugged. 'I knew the answer, anyway. Don't worry about it. We'll go another time.'

'Yes, of course,' she promised.

'I shall go,' he added. 'They'll be disappointed that you couldn't be there for the boy's birthday party—but I'll explain that it was difficult for you to get away.'

She watched him walk down the path and her eyes were troubled. He turned at the gate and lifted a hand in salute as was his custom. She waved in return and closed the door as he climbed into the old car and slammed the car door behind him. She knew that he was hurt, more by her forgetfulness of the outing to his sister's home than by her failure to keep the date. She thought ruefully that her dates with Frank could never mean very much to her for she gave them little thought and without his reminders would forget them completely. She decided to try to make amends in some way. She was really sorry to disappoint him for he showed them a great many kindnesses and throughout the years had been a staunch friend and a help to them in many ways.

Michael was yawning widely when Isobel returned to the sitting-room. It was much later than his usual bedtime and within a few minutes Isobel had made up a bed for him on the sofa and sent him off to wash and undress. She quickly made cocoa for them all and

Michael sat on the rug before the fire, a mug of cocoa in his hand, his cheeks glowing, partly from the firelight and partly from a vigorous scrubbing with soap and water. His auburn hair was tumbled and gleaming brightly.

Isobcl bent over her small brother and made his covers secure. Then she kissed his forehead and left him to sleep. He fell asleep with the swift ease of childhood, one arm lying over the top of the blankets, his bright hair almost hidden as he lay burrowed down in his natural sleeping position.

They talked quietly, seated around the glowing fire, and their voices did not disturb him. Before long, however, Lisa began to look weary and Isobcl insisted that she should go to bed. A little reluctantly, she at last agreed and Desmond swung her up into his strong arms and carried her into the small, neat bedroom. Then he left the two sisters together. Isobel quickly helped Lisa to undress, brought water for her to wash, and tucked her between the sheets with the same maternal solicitude that she had shown to Michael. She kissed Lisa's cheek and her sister clung to her with unusual affection. Isobel waited a moment, wondering if Lisa wanted to say anything to her about Desmond, but she waited in vain.

Lisa lay back on her pillows, the golden hair streaming about her sweet face, 'Send Desmond in to say good night,' she said gently.

'Of course I will,' Isobel promised and went

back to the sitting-room. Desmond was standing in front of the fire, smoking a cigarette, his expression thoughtful. He glanced at Isobel as she entered. 'Will you go and say good night to Lisa?' she asked. He nodded and went from the room. It seemed a long time before he returned and she wondered what was passing between them. At last he came in and smiled at her. He sat down before the fire and picked up the poker. Absently, he poked the glowing embers. Isobel picked up some sewing she had been working on and began to stitch away at it. There was a silence between them and she wondered at his thoughts. Her own were of him and Lisa.

He turned from the fire and looked at her. The soft light gave her a new beauty, a luminous beauty, and his heart began to pound unexpectedly. He leaned across and laid his hand on hers. She looked up, dropping the sewing. 'Come and sit with me,' he invited. Obediently and without question, she rose and sat down on the rug at his feet. He touched her silken hair, short and tumbling riotously over her head. She raised her face and smiled tremulously at him. He said abruptly, 'I wonder if you know how much I appreciate the welcome you always give me and the warmth of your friendship.'

'I think I do,' she said slowly. 'But we're all very fond of you, Desmond—you're accepted as one of the family by us all.' She laughed softly. 'It might sound a little strange when we've known each other such a short time—but time has very little to do with it.'

He stroked the fair curls with a gentle hand. 'I'm very fond of you,' he said.

She felt her heart catch at the words. He had not said 'all of you' but simply 'you' and she wondered if he realized this or whether he had said it deliberately. Suddenly she felt very close to this man. Perhaps it was the light touch of his hand on her hair. Perhaps it was his low tones which seemed to engulf them both in a sweet intimacy which no other person could share. Perhaps it was the gentle flicker of the firelight and the cosy atmosphere of the attractive room. She could not define it but she knew instinctively that his heart thudded in the same way as her own heart, that he knew too the sense of familiar intimacy between them, that he sought something which only she could give him—but her mind refused to frame the word. Only her heart's swift tattoo was rebellious.

His hand strayed to her shoulder and the slight pressure turned her slight body towards him. For a moment she resisted but the appeal in his eyes could not be denied. She turned to him. Raising her hands to his dark head, she lowered it and kissed him lightly on the lips. His arms went about her but when he would have drawn her close to him, she shook her head. With a swift movement, she was on her feet, looking down at him.

'Good night, Desmond,' she said quietly. He caught her hand and lifted it to his lips almost reverently. Her smile curved her lips with sweetness and her eyes were very warm.

'Don't go,' he said in a low voice. 'I want to talk to you.'

She kept her tone deliberately light. 'Can't it keep till the morning? You know which is your room, don't you?'

He nodded. 'I shall have a last cigarette before I go to bed,' he told her. She released her hand from his strong clasp. 'Stay and have one with me,' he suggested quickly. 'I really do want to talk to you, Isobel—about Lisa.' He noticed the light which flashed to her eyes and he thought to himself that it was a protective gleam as though he threatened to attack her young. It struck him forcibly that she had always had to be more maternal than anything else in her relationship with her brother and sister.

She sat down, albeit a little reluctantly, in her former armchair and absently picked up the sewing, folding it neatly and putting it away. Desmond took out his cigarette-case and offered it to her, Isobel shook her head and he helped himself. As he flicked his lighter into life, she said, 'What about Lisa?'

He said abruptly, 'I see that Lisa keeps that book of poems beside her bed—open at the poem I marked.'

112

Isobel spoke lightly. 'It happens to be one of her favourites—it seems you have similar tastes, Desmond.'

'So she told me,' he replied.

'Why did you mark it?' she asked unexpectedly, surprising herself. She knew it was a question better left unasked but the words had come of their own volition.

He paused a moment. At last he said: 'I've had that book a long time, Isobel. The first time I met you I thought of that particular poem. When I returned to London I looked it up and marked it so that whenever I opened the book it would remind me of you.' He smiled warmly into her eyes. 'Not that I need a poem as a reminder,' he said frankly. 'I carry the memory of you with me all the time.'

Her face clouded at his words. He was taken aback by her expression of dismay. He had been so sure that she would be touched and pleased—this pain in her eyes was unexpected and bewildering. But Isobel had known a moment's swift joy and then her first thought was for Lisa and her sister's love for this man. It was incredible that Desmond should care for her—what else could she read into his words—but it was also impossible. Lisa's happiness must always come before her own.

'But you sent the book of poems to Lisa,' she reminded him.

So this was the reason for her pain. He said quickly, 'I thought she would enjoy reading them—I know she loves poetry. But I hoped you would see that marked passage and know it was meant for you, Isobel. We understand each other—you're a sensitive person and I thought you knew how I felt about you. Words didn't seem necessary.' He smiled across at her. 'You knew I was coming today but I gave you no warning. Isn't that enough evidence that you are attuned to my thoughts?'

She was silent, confused. He searched her eyes and perhaps he read her thoughts for he said suddenly, 'Did Lisa think I meant those words for her?'

She found it impossible to lie. 'Yes,' she said quietly.

His expression was troubled. 'Then that's what she meant when she said how happy the gift had made her. Does she care for me, Isobel?' He asked the question with trepidation in his voice. At her nod, he caught his breath sharply. Then he added very gently: 'And you? You do care for me too, don't you? I've always known it.'

Isobel made up her mind swiftly. Whatever it cost her, she could not take Desmond from her sister—and if she denied the love in her own heart, then perhaps Lisa's love would in time stir a response in Desmond's being.

'I'm going to marry Frank,' she said firmly. 'I should have told you before—it's been settled a long time.' Perhaps it was not a lie, she told herself against the rebellion in her heart. She had always known that Frank cared for her and wanted to marry her. They knew each other so well and surely friendship was a good basis for marriage. Frank was a fine man, steady and reliable and kind. They would know a certain happiness although she might never know the wild, rapturous joy that life with Desmond Crane could bring her.

He was stunned. He knew now why the farmer had been hostile to him. But he could not believe that Isobel was in love with Frank. He was convinced that he would have sensed any such emotion in her. But he also felt sure that she would not lie to him. If she said she was going to marry the farmer, then that was her intention—but all of his being cried out against the denial of the rare and wonderful affinity which he knew existed between himself and this woman 'of fair and shining beauty'.

CHAPTER EIGHT

Desmond stacked the wet dishes on the draining board, whistling merrily. Isobel wiped them and put them away carefully, She had tied an apron about his waist much to his disgust but he gave in without too much protest. It was many years since he had washed up after a meal but he enjoyed the self-imposed task, even refusing Isobel's offer to tackle the dirty saucepans.

Isobel could not resist a smile as she worked beside him. She had accepted his offer of help with alacrity, prompted more by a sense of mischief than the real need for his help in the kitchen. But he was proving himself quite capable of the task and she knew he was quite happy. There was a homely atmosphere and a sense of long familiarity between them.

The dishes washed, he untied the apron and threw it over the back of a chair. He sat on the edge of the table and folded his arms on his chest as Isobel filled the kettle and set it on the gas cooker. She set out tea things and he sighed a little sigh.

'Methinks there will be more washing up in the near future,' he said lightly.

Isobel laughed. 'There always is,' she told him. 'Eating is a necessity that even the scientists haven't done away with yet.'

'Tablets are the thing,' he assured her with mock solemnity. 'I never eat anything else at home. But I always think it's a pity that Hastings has to lay up a table with gleaming silver and cutlery and spotless napery so that I can sit down to my three-course tablet meal at eight o'clock precisely every night.'

Isobel threw him a laughing, reproachful glance for his teasing. 'Then why not do away with the formality?'

He raised his eyebrows in mock horror. 'My dear girl—England is built on its traditions!

116

Do you want us to become a nation of people hastily swallowing our tablets with a glass of water at odd hours of the day?'

She aimed a light blow at his chin with her fist. 'Fool!' she derided. He caught her hand swiftly and held it. For a long moment she stood close to him while he held her hand— she looked up at him with affectionate warmth in her eyes and he caught his breath. Confusion swept over her then she hastily released herself. 'The kettle is boiling,' she announced. 'Go into the sitting-room—I'll bring in the tray. We've left the others alone too long.'

Without a word he obeyed her. She looked after him—at the broad back, the proud poise of the dark head, the swift ease of his lithe movements—and it was well for his peace of mind that he could not see the expression on her fair, flower-like face.

They were very good friends and he came often to the little white house. But no mention was ever made by either of them to the conversation they had shared that Saturday night already three months away. He had accepted her firm explanation that she was going to marry Frank Cummins—but acceptance had not been easy. He had tried to deny the love in his heart but this too had not been easy and there were times when he longed to crush her to him and insist that she loved him as much as he loved her.

117

Isobel had fought the weary battle with herself over and over again, Occasionally she longed to surrender to her emotions and run into Desmond's arms. But always she remembered Lisa whose love for Desmond was as strong as ever although it remained unspoken. It seemed to Isobel that her sister had a right to happiness—more right than any woman who had so much else in life. Lisa had so little and she was so good and innocent and as fair inwardly as outwardly. If anyone deserved happiness, then Lisa did. So she welcomed Desmond to the house and they had achieved a warm friendly footing which was never abused by a careless word or glance. Isobel hoped with all her heart that in time Desmond would realize that his love was hopeless and would turn to Lisa.

He was kind and affectionate to Lisa, generous in many ways: they were happy with each other. Desmond saw in Lisa many of Isobel's qualities and he was very fond of her, But no one in his right senses could imagine his feelings for Lisa to approach a lover-like attitude.

Lisa's own simplicity enabled her to understand the situation. She knew that Desmond cared for her sister: she sensed that Isobel responded in the depths of her secret heart. But it was apparent that Isobel had a reason for not encouraging Desmond's attentions. It was Lisa's simplicity too which prevented her from realizing that she was the reason. If she wondered about Isobel's reluctance to admit her emotions and to give herself up to the happiness which Desmond would so readily offer, then she assumed that Isobel felt herself unable to desert her sister and Michael by marriage. Lisa was troubled by this loyalty while she understood it. She could see no way out of Isobel's difficulties. Michael was still only a child and he needed Isobel. But Desmond was devoted to the boy and surely he would take over the responsibilities of his welfare if he married Isobel. Lisa told herself sadly that she was the main drawback. No man could be expected to provide for his wife's invalid sister indefinitely. He would resent the necessary attention which she demanded of Isobel. Any marriage between Desmond and her sister must start off on a poor footing unless there were some way in which Isobel could be relieved of the burden of her sister and brother.

Lisa turned the problem over and over in her mind but she could never find a solution. She was familiar with the hardest lesson in life—that of acceptance—so eventually she realized that only time would solve this problem and there was nothing she could do to further matters. She was willing to sacrifice her own heart for Isobel's sake—her love for Desmond had not lessened and his presence was a bitter-sweet joy to her. But she possessed a great humility and it was no surprise to her that Desmond did not love her in return. She adored her sister and would gladly bring about her happiness if it were within her power. So she waited. One day, she felt sure, she would have the opportunity to help Isobel to gain her heart's desire.

All this was instinctive on her part. Isobel never spoke of her love for Desmond. He never betrayed his feelings. There were no secret exchange of glances, no casual words with a deeper meaning, no attempts to capture a few sweet moments alone. When he came to the house, it was always Lisa who knew his kindnesses, his thoughtfulness, his tender solicitude. He sought her company and beguiled her with interesting conversations, humorous entertainment and his fascinating descriptions of London life and bustle.

Isobel occupied herself with many things and endeavoured to leave Lisa and Desmond alone for as long as possible. She hoped to foster an intimacy between them which would develop into mutual love based on friendship. She hoped for the happiness which she knew marriage would bring to Lisa. She told herself that Desmond too would be happy for Lisa was lovely, talented and intelligent: she was amusing and gay; she was sweet and honest and appealing. There was no reason in the world why Desmond should not come to love her as much as she loved him. She dismissed the idea that he was the kind of man who only loved once and he had already found the woman to stir that emotion in him. She reminded herself that he had never actually said that he loved her—she would not admit that she had not given him the time, or that he had said that words were not necessary between them. If there were times when her heart lifted because of his presence and she knew that a chord in him responded to the tumult of her blood, then she pushed those times from her memory and strengthened her determination to refute her love.

She was thankful for one thing: although she had told Desmond that she meant to marry Frank and that it was all settled, she still waited for Frank to speak of marriage to her. It was a relief that he was so patient and unassuming. She was determined to keep to her decision. At least one man would be happy—and she knew that she would make Frank a good wife. He was a simple man and it needed little to make him content. Isobel clung to the thought of marrying him because she knew it was her only defence against the love which stirred her entire being. He was a raft in the sea of heady emotion and she told herself that in time she would learn to love Frank—not in the way that she loved Desmond, but a more peaceful, steadier and perhaps more worthwhile love. Frank would never regret their marriage. She was determined to have no regrets either. All her life, Isobel had been possessed of courage—not the courage necessary to do daring, reckless deeds in time of danger—but a steady, simple courage which carried her through times of trouble. It had always been necessary for her to hold her head high, keep a smile on her lips and a brightness in her eyes, to forge ahead without fear through life. Since she had been left to care for Lisa and Michael, her courage had stood her in good stead. They had needed her and turned to her instinctively—she had never failed them. She had always made sacrifices for their sake—it was a natural duty made very sweet by her love for them both.

So she accepted that it was her duty to ensure Lisa's happiness before her own—and she knew that if she succeeded, she would know enough reward because she had not failed her sister in the most important way of all.

As they sat over tea in the sitting-room, Desmond said suddenly, 'My visit this time was for a purpose—I'm combining business with pleasure.'

Isobel looked up inquiringly. 'Well?'

'I want to talk to you about Michael. How old is he now—eleven?'

Lisa nodded. 'He was eleven last month.' She smiled warmly at him. 'You surely remember his birthday—you brought him his electric train set!'

He went on, 'It's a great pleasure to me to give him presents. But I want to do something much more lasting for him—something that goes much further than the occasional gift. Isobel, you're his guardian. Will you allow me to send him to a good school and pay for his education? He has a good brain and is willing to learn. The village school may be an excellent institution but it is surely very cramping for a boy of his intelligence.'

Isobel was startled by this further demonstration of his generosity. Startled and a little reluctant to agree. Michael was her responsibility—but she could not help but see the common sense in Desmond's argument. He was an intelligent child with a great love for learning. It had always been his ambition to go away to school so that one day he could go on to college. It would be a great thing for him and would be of lasting benefit. A surge of gratitude brought a swift light to her eyes.

She was silent so long that Desmond said at last, 'I really want to do this for him, Isobel. I'm very fond of Michael—he's a fine boy and I think he should have the advantages that I can give him.'

'Desmond, it's a wonderful idea,' Lisa said swiftly. 'How like you to think of it! Michael will be thrilled—and very grateful to you.'

He laid a hand over hers. 'Isobel hasn't agreed yet,' he reminded her.

'I don't know what to say,' Isobel said slowly. 'It's a wonderful gesture on your part—and further proof of your kindness.' She paused, searching for the right words. 'I do agree that Michael needs a better education than the village school can provide. I do agree that it will help in many ways in the future. But, Desmond—he isn't your responsibility. There's no reason why you should do this for him.'

'This isn't a wild impulse on my part,' he told her firmly. 'I've been thinking about it for several weeks.'

'But surely it will be a terrible expense,' Isobel protested. 'He's only eleven—it means at least five or six years at school.'

Desmond shrugged. 'I can well afford the expense. I hope he will go on to college eventually. If he doesn't get a scholarship then I'm fully prepared to pay for that providing he lives up to my expectations of him. I think he will work hard and prove that all the expense is worth while.'

Isobel still hesitated. 'I can't say yes without thinking seriously about it. I do appreciate your desire to help him, Desmond . . .'

'Then why hesitate?' he asked quickly. 'You haven't put forward any good reasons why you should refuse my offer, you know.'

'If you were a relative . . .' Isobel began.

'What difference does that make?' he demanded. 'You've said often enough that you think of me as one of the family—now you're treating me like a complete outsider.' There was a hint of resentment in his tone.

'I understand how Isobel feels,' Lisa said gently. 'We do think of you as one of the family, Desmond—but the fact remains that Michael's education could prove very expensive for you and it would seem a terrible imposition on our part. We could never hope to repay you—and it seems too much to ask of you.'

Resentment faded from his expression as he listened to her simple explanation. It was replaced by a warm eagerness. 'How could it possibly be an imposition? I can never repay you for all you've done for me these last few months. It's been wonderful to know your friendship and your affection. You've always made me welcome and treated me like a lifelong friend. I can never hope to emphasize how grateful I am to you all. All I can do is to show my gratitude in some way—and right now, the way is to send Michael to school. I think the expense will be justified. I hope some day to be very proud of him—and my pride will be all the greater because I shall know that I've had a hand in forming the man he will become. Please don't deny me this opportunity to do something, not only for Michael, but for you too, Isobel,' He added quietly, 'You must have often worried about his future—I'd like to take that worry away from you. Will you let me?'

Isobel smiled and nodded. 'Very well, Desmond. But we can never thank you enough.'

'Don't try to thank me,' he said quickly. 'I don't want any thanks. It will be ample reward to see Michael's face when he hears the news.' From the light in his eyes, Isobel and Lisa knew that he spoke sincerely and they exchanged glances. He went on: 'I hope this will be only the first of the many things I'd like to do for you—it will make me very happy to give you pleasure, you know.' He spoke to both women yet his eyes rested briefly on Isobel's sober face.

Later he said, 'I've already made a few tentative inquiries. I went to a very good school in Scotland and I know they would take him—I've a special reason for wanting Michael to go there. I always said that my son would follow in my footsteps—well, I haven't a son to send. I think of Michael very much in the light of a son—so it seems the obvious choice.'

Isobel felt a few misgivings—Scotland was a long way off and she wondered if Michael would be homesick and perhaps unhappy—he had never been away from home before—the school was a famous name and undoubtedly expensive.

She said, 'It must entail a great many expenses besides the fees, Desmond. Clothes

126

and books and sports gear, I suppose.'

'Don't worry about anything,' he said, 'I'll bear all expenses.'

At last Isobel cast aside her misgivings. She could not turn down such a wonderful opportunity for Michael. She waited until Desmond wrote to tell her that he had made all the arrangements and Michael would start the new term in a few weeks' time. Michael's joy knew no bounds when Isobel eventually broke the news to him.

He stood and stared at her, his face suddenly pale and his eyes suspiciously bright. There was a tensity in his slight body and his hands were clenched until the fingernails dug sharply into his palms.

'You really mean it? I'm going away to school?'

Isobel looked swiftly at his face. There was a strange note in his voice. She drew him quickly to her and held him close. 'You don't have to go, Michael,' she reassured him. 'If you'd rather stay here with us . . .'

'I want to go,' he said firmly. 'It's the most wonderfullest thing that ever happened to me.' Standing in the circle of her arms, he looked up at her. 'But I thought we couldn't afford to send me to school, Isobel.'

She hesitated, wondering whether he should know the truth. But she had never lied to him. So now she said quietly, 'Desmond is paying your school fees, Michael. It's a very kind

127

gesture and I'm afraid we really should have refused his offer—but I know how much you've always wanted to go away to a good school and it's a wonderful opportunity for you.'

He was very silent. He searched her eyes. At last he said very softly, 'I bet he'd make a wonderful father, Isobel.'

She hugged him. 'It's because he hasn't any sons of his own that he wants to do so much for you,' she told him.

'He really is one of the family now,' he said and at last delight was seeping in, taking the place of incredulous wonderment in his eyes. He released himself from Isobel's arms and ran from the room. She watched him go, wondering if he was perilously near tears and reluctant to cry in her presence for he liked to think of himself as manly. But Michael sped out into the garden where he relieved his emotional tension by racing round and round the house on the concrete path until a thought struck him and he came back into the house in search of the model aeroplane which had been Desmond's first gift to him. It was looking a little battered now for it had been flown several times from Brierly Hill and had occasionally come to grief. But it was Michael's most treasured possession, valued even above the magnificent electric train set which had been his unexpected birthday present from Desmond. He crept away into a

128

secluded corner of the garden which was his private 'den'. He held the plane very close to him, thinking his own thoughts—strangely mature thoughts for a boy of his age. He knew that he was extremely fortunate that Desmond Crane had made the sudden turn of events possible. He knew that all his life he would have cause to thank Desmond for his generosity yet he knew too that the man would not want any verbal thanks. He determined to do his best at the new school so that Desmond would have his reward in his progress and quick learning, so that Desmond could be proud to have helped him to further a dream which he had possessed for the last two years.

CHAPTER NINE

A little repentant of his recent neglect where Helen was concerned, Desmond waited for an answer to his ring at her doorbell.

Helen herself came to the door. She opened it wide at sight of him and her eyes were warm with pleasure. 'Desmond! You're almost a stranger—come in, my dear.'

She closed the door behind him and he looked down at her. His smile was a little rueful. 'You must find me a most unpredictable person,' he said. 'It's weeks since I saw you—but I do apologize sincerely,

129

Helen.'

She linked her hand in his arm and drew him into the lounge. 'Don't worry about it,' she assured him. 'I expect you've been busy—but I must say that I fully expected you to be at George's dinner party last week.'

'I was in France,' he said. 'An old friend of mine telephoned me with an invitation to spend a few days with him at his villa near Cannes—I needed a brief holiday and he made the place sound irresistible. What have you been doing with yourself, Helen, anyway—I don't think you've lacked for eligible escorts, have you?' His eyes twinkled down at her. A smile curved his lips as a very faint blush tinged her cheeks.

'I've been caught up in the usual social round,' she replied easily but she made no answer to his subtle prompt about her escorts. She was looking very beautiful in a flame coloured evening dress which clung to her slim figure, revealing and emphasizing the exquisite contours of her youthful body. Desmond was again conscious of her beauty but he compared it with the fair innocence of the Lomax sisters—and a shaft of pain caught at his heart for it was several weeks now since he had been back to the little white house. He lived with a constant pain because Isobel was lost to him—and there was in him an innate kindness which prevented him from encouraging the swift, impetuous flame of love in Lisa's heart. So he

130

stayed away. Helen added, 'I'm glad you came, my dear—but I'm afraid I'm going out very shortly. Why didn't you telephone me?'

'I should have done,' he admitted. 'But this is only a passing visit—I came to ask you to dine with me tomorrow evening.' She accepted with alacrity and he added, 'You're looking very nice in all your finery. That's a new gown, isn't it?'

'Observant Desmond!' she teased him. 'Yes, it's new—but I think that must be the first time you've ever noticed my clothes. What's happened to sharpen your observation, my dear?' She did not wait for his reply. She had not expected one, anyway. Helen moved to the cocktail cabinet with the flowing ease of movement which was characteristic of the woman. She poured drinks for them both and offered Desmond a cigarette from the cedarwood box. They exchanged light conversation and while they talked, Helen studied him and her eyes were thoughtful. She still felt a surge of warm affection for him but she realized now that it had never been anything deeper than affection. She had long since admitted to herself that she loved Ryan Nesbit with every fibre of her being. But she kept her secrets. Occasionally they met and he was a good companion: he was the escort she waited for now. She had found out so many things about him which only endeared him to her even more. He was happy with her and valued their friendship but there was no hint that it would ever become anything more. She still had not found any way to overcome the pride which was so great a part of his character. He had managed to get another job and, to her relief, was sticking at it with dogged determination but he never ceased to chafe against restriction and long to break free. He still lived in his South London digs but he had never allowed Helen to visit him there. Whenever they met, it was at a public restaurant or at her flat. They did not meet enough for Helen's contentment. But she had to accept Ryan for the man he was and his pride was not a thing she could dismiss lightly. If only there were some way in which she could help him without attacking that pride . . . Suddenly an idea came to her. If she confided in Desmond, who would understand and appreciate the finer points of the relationship between Ryan and herself, perhaps he could find a solution—or he might offer some useful advice. He was a man of the world. Moreover, he was a man's man and must have met many of Ryan's calibre.

She touched Desmond's hand. 'Desmond, in a few minutes a friend of mine will be calling for me. I want you to meet him.'

Desmond raised an eyebrow. Her tone was a little breathless as though she had been plucking up courage to speak the words and then poured them out impulsively.

'Tell me about him?' he invited, realizing that Helen had mentioned her escort for a reason.

She paused a moment, then said, 'His name is Ryan Nesbit—he's a little younger than me but a very fine person.' She smiled briefly. 'When you see him, you'll probably wonder why I'm going out with him because he's totally different to any of the other men who have been my escorts in the past. He's tall and big—big in the powerful sense of the word. He isn't remarkably handsome—simply nice and pleasant-faced. He's a little shy and yet terribly self-possessed . . .' She broke off.

'Where did you meet him?' Desmond asked with a stirring of interest. There was a light in Helen's eyes as she spoke of the man which he had never seen before. It disturbed him a little.

This time the blush swept across her skin and this disturbed him even more for she had never been a woman to blush easily. She replied in a tone that was faintly hesitant, 'Well, rather oddly, as a matter of fact. We bumped into each other in the street—we started to talk—well, it just seemed that we were meant to meet and make friends.'

Desmond's eyebrows climbed very high. 'How very like you, my dear Helen!' he exclaimed and there was almost a note of censure.

She hastened to defend herself, 'Yes, I knew you'd think it impetuous of me, as usual, But really, he was so nice and I liked him on sight. He really isn't the type of man who normally picks up a woman in the street,' she added quickly.

Desmond sighed, 'My God, Helen, I sometimes think you need a nursemaid—even at your age. I've warned you times without number against these odd acquaintances you seem to pick up in bars and public parks and shops. What do you know about this man, anyway, apart from his name?'

Helen was too used to Desmond to take offence at his words. She knew he merely had her interests at heart. She knew too that he had been right in the past about the unsavouriness of some of the characters she had met and 'liked on sight'. For all her twenty-eight years, she admitted to a certain naïve impulsiveness. She was very fortunate in that it had never yet landed her in trouble—but mainly because Desmond usually sifted the wheat from the chaff and advised her on her friendships.

So she replied easily, 'Oh, he's an artist.'

With a swift flash of humour, Desmond said lightly, 'Not the pavement type, I hope?'

She laughed and immediately the atmosphere seemed to lighten and she knew that now she could talk about Ryan with ease and sure confidence of his understanding,

'You're jumping to conclusions because I met him in the street,' she said, helping herself to a cigarette. Their eyes met and his twinkled merrily. 'He's a fine artist, Desmond—he really has a great gift. He's working in an office during the day but he hates it—he wants time and freedom to paint. He's poor and terribly proud—he hates my money and I'm afraid it creates rather a barrier between us.' Momentarily her eyes were sad. 'There isn't any way I can help him yet I want to so much. I wish you'd tell me what I can do, Desmond.'

He searched her face. 'Is he really any good as a painter? Have you seen any of his work?'

'Oh yes,' she assured him eagerly. 'He brought a few canvases to show me—they are good! Very good! I may not know very much about art but I do know when a painting puts over its subject with feeling . . .' She broke off and shrugged helplessly. 'I can't explain myself very well—but if you had seen them, you would know what I mean.'

Her intensity touched him and he wondered at the relationship between Helen and the young artist. With his swift insight, it was not difficult to sense that she cared for Nesbit—or thought she did. But he had experienced her swift interest in new friends before—and also experienced their swift deaths when she had found out all there was to know about them and they began to bore her. He wondered if this friendship would follow the usual course. But he admitted to himself that Helen spoke with an eager intensity which he had never heard before—and he could not deny that her eyes shone with a new warm light. Perhaps this time a friendship would last and ripen into something warmer. He was devoted to Helen and he knew she was unhappy at heart, although gay and careless superficially. She was unhappy for she sought a happiness which had always been denied to her—but perhaps this artist could bring it to her . . .

So he said, 'Well, I shall enjoy meeting your artist friend—I'll soon sum him up and I'll let you know if you're being played for a sucker again or not. After all, Helen—and I've told you this before—you're an extremely wealthy woman, besides being very attractive. There are a great many unscrupulous young rogues about these days—Nesbit's pride could be a pretence in order to enlist your help. There are many ways a man can take to part an impulsive woman from her money—and you won't deny the impulsive part, my dear, I know.'

Her face clouded a little. 'I can't believe that of Ryan,' she said stubbornly. 'I know he's sincere and fine all the way through.' She looked down at her lovely hands. She twisted a cigarette round and round between the slim fingers. Without meeting his eyes, she said in a low voice, 'I'm in love with him, Desmond. It isn't a youthful infatuation this time—nor is it misguided desire to help someone not as fortunate as myself. I love Ryan Nesbit—I would marry him tomorrow if only he'd give me the chance—and if I found out that he is only interested in my money . . . well, it wouldn't make any difference. I'd marry Ryan on any terms!'

The sense of shock that flooded Desmond convinced him that Helen spoke the truth. But before he could muster a reply, the door bell shrilled and she leaped to her feet, stubbing her cigarette swiftly. Desmond watched her as she hastened across the room, her whole body filled with eagerness. He sat back comfortably, listening as she opened the front door. Without straining his ears deliberately, he could hear the exchange of greetings.

Ryan Nesbit said, 'Am I late? I usually am.'

'It doesn't matter,' she assured him. 'Come in, Ryan.'

'I hope you don't want to go anywhere too ritzy,' he said diffidently. 'I didn't realize you were dressing up—I would have borrowed my pal's tuxedo. This suit is rather inappropriate for a night-club.'

'You're always worrying about appearances,' she chided him. She dismissed his claim to poverty and pushed aside the little irritation that such reminders always brought, to her mind. 'Come into the lounge. An old friend of mine is waiting to meet you, Ryan.'

As they entered the lounge, Desmond got to his feet. While he smiled politely, waiting for Helen to make the necessary introduction, his

137

keen eyes scanned the big young man. His first impression was one of surprised pleasure. From past experience, he had assumed the worst but this latest addition to Helen's collection of 'friendships' was a pleasant-faced, tall and broad-shouldered young man with an easy smile and an ease of movement despite his powerful build. The two men looked at each other, weighing up. Then Helen said quickly, 'Desmond Crane—Ryan Nesbit. I'll get you a drink, Ryan. Desmond, another drink?'

'Thanks.' Desmond shook hands with the younger man. Nesbit's clasp was firm and reassuring. They smiled at each other and Desmond knew immediately why Helen had been swept off her feet by the artist. His smile was frank and warm, his eyes candid.

He said, 'I'm very pleased to meet you, Mr. Crane. Helen has mentioned you several times. I believe you're friends of long standing.'

Desmond grinned. 'We've known each other many years. Helen has told me a little about you. You're an artist, I understand?'

Ryan nodded. He sat down in an armchair and crossed one leg over the other. His fingers began to beat a restless tattoo on the arm of the chair as he replied. 'A poor and struggling artist.'

'I'm told that all the best artists starved in a garret,' Desmond returned easily.

'Too right! My digs very much resemble the legendary garret.' He took the glass which Helen offered with a smile for her eyes alone. 'But at the moment I'm earning a pittance in the insurance business.'

'I should like to see some of your work,' Desmond said, twisting the glass in his fingers and studying the contents.

'Perhaps we could arrange for you to bring some canvases here,' Helen put in. 'Desmond takes a great interest in art, you know—although he's primarily a writer and publisher.'

There was a hint of reproach in Ryan's voice. 'I recognized the name, of course. I've read one or two of your books.' He turned to Desmond. 'I shall be pleased to show you some of my efforts—an unbiased opinion is always valuable.'

'He means that my opinion isn't unbiased,' Helen said quickly. 'Neither is it particularly valuable as I'm not really a connoisseur of art.'

'Have you any particular style for subjects?' Desmond asked slowly.

Ryan shrugged. 'Child studies—portraits—landscapes—they're all the same to me.'

They talked of art for a few minutes then Desmond drained his glass and rose. 'Well, I must be on my way. Thanks for the drinks, Helen.' He held out his hand to Nesbit. 'It was most interesting to meet you, Nesbit. I shall look forward to a second meeting and the opportunity of seeing your work.'

Helen saw Desmond out of the flat and promised to telephone him when she had arranged for Ryan to bring the canvases. Then she added quickly, 'Well, Desmond? What did you think of Ryan?'

Desmond smiled down at her. 'Is my opinion valuable?' he teased. Then he said, 'Your taste is improving, my dear Helen. The man has charm and personality. What is more important—he has breeding. Do you know anything about his family?'

'Only that his mother was Irish. I'm so glad that you like him—I should have been terribly disappointed if you didn't. Do you think there's any way to help him—get him out of that boring office and give him freedom to work? I know he could be a successful artist if he had the time to paint—but I'm sure the atmosphere of his digs must be terribly cramping.'

Desmond would not commit himself yet. 'Well, I'll see,' he compromised. 'I expect something can be done—and if he really has any talent, then something must be done. But I'd like to know more about his background— what he's done with his life until now.'

Helen glanced at her watch. 'There isn't time to go into details here and now. But I'll telephone you, Desmond—and then we can talk about him at length.'

He bent his head and kissed her brow, as was his habit 'I thought you were dining with me tomorrow night? We can talk then.'

'Oh, of course. Call for me at eight, will you?'

She closed the door on him and then returned to the lounge. Ryan was standing by the window, one hand raised in support against the wall, his mid-brown hair falling across the sensitive brow. He turned his head at Helen's entry and she walked across the room to join him.

'I like your friend,' he said and slipped his arm about her shoulders in a casual gesture. 'He's no fool. He knows a great deal about art, that's evident.'

'That's why I wanted you to meet him, Ryan,' she said gently.

He threw her a suspicious look. 'Are you cooking something up with him? You'd go to any lengths to give me a helping hand—I know that. You know I won't accept any help from you. I suppose you think that Crane might be more subtle and more persuasive?'

Anger sparked in her. 'Desmond has a great many contacts and he could be a great help to you.'

He shook his head stubbornly. 'If I can't make the grade by myself, then I'm not much of an artist. I don't need any boost from anyone.'

She shrugged his arm from her shoulders with an impatient movement. Moving away from him, she helped herself to a cigarette and

141

flicked a lighter into life with hands that trembled slightly.

'I hate your independence!' she snapped. 'One day you might realize that other people are necessary in your life. One day you might wake up to the knowledge that it's impossible to do anything or get anywhere without a helping hand from someone!'

'Independence is a great thing,' he replied slowly. 'You've always had someone to look after you and provide everything you've expressed a wish for, Helen. You're spoilt and selfish and wilful—and you expect me and everyone else to fall in with your plans and wishes. I'm not going to let you run my life. I'm sorry—but I've always done that for myself and I'm not doing so badly. I appreciate your interest and your friendship—but I prefer to keep my independence. I've only found one person to be necessary in my life—my mother who brought me into the world and guided my infant steps. As soon as I was old enough to think for myself, I knew what I wanted to do and I set about doing it. If I can't get what I want on my own, then I'd rather go without it. I don't paint to sell my work, you know. It's my life.'

Helen's face was drained of all colour. His words had hurt. She repeated them now. 'Spoilt, selfish and wilful—is that how you think of me?'

'Well, aren't you? Spoilt by indulgent

parents, selfish because you can afford to be and wilful because you've always gone after what you wanted and managed to get it— mostly with the money which has always surrounded you.'

'You're being brutally frank,' she murmured, fighting against the pain which held her in a violent grip.

'Yes, I suppose I am,' he admitted. 'But that's my nature—you should know that by now, Helen.'

She was silent for a moment. His quiet but firm remarks still echoed in her brain. With a spurt of anger. she said, 'I'm not trying to run your life. I know that you're a fine artist and I want to see you make a success with your paintings. If Desmond or anyone else can make it possible, then why shouldn't I interest them in you and your work?'

'Because I don't want you to create opportunities for me,' he returned swiftly. 'If my work is any good then it will find its own success. If it doesn't, then I shall be content to go on painting for my own enjoyment and creative outlet. Money and success don't particularly appeal to me. Freedom of movement and from conventionality are my only aims—anything that restricts either, I shall cut out of my life.' He moved towards her. 'I'm sorry if I've hurt you, Helen—it's quite unintentional. I just want to impress upon you that I don't want or need your help or anyone else's help!' He put his hand on her shoulder.

'How evil pride can be!' Helen flashed, and she threw off his gentle hand.

He stood looking down at her for a long moment. Then he said, 'This is the first time we've quarrelled, Helen. I thought you understood how I feel—it seems I took your understanding for granted. I'm sorry. Shall I go?'

Because of her disappointment and anger, she knew a swift impulse to send him away. But her love for him swept through her as their eyes met and she knew she could not. She shook her head. 'No, Ryan. Let's forget and forgive the harsh words.'

For answer he took her into his arms and held her close, making no attempt to kiss her, but holding her against his hard chest, his fair cheek against the raven hair. His thoughts were in turmoil. He knew he had been brutally frank. He had his reasons for this. Although he had never spoken of it, he had a very real love for this woman who, despite her wealth and sophistication and self-indulgence, had many saving graces. But that same wealth and sophistication created a barrier between them—and Ryan felt in his heart that no amount of mutual love could ever entirely rid them of that barrier. He knew that he had too much pride. He knew that he would never ask Helen to marry him simply because of that pride. Of

144

late he had been tormented with the desire to be with her always mingled with the longing to walk out of her life now before he was entirely lost in a welter of emotion. She had been angry at his words and she had every right to be so—pride was the besetting sin yet he was unable to conquer it. He had given her an opportunity to end their friendship—and now he was thankful that she had not taken it. Unsatisfactory though their relationship might be, at least he could see her occasionally, talk to her, be with her. This was no love affair that could be banished from one's system with time. It was a real and lasting love—and Ryan admitted to himself that his work had improved with the quickening of his emotions. He could wish that they were able to spend their lives together, knowing that Helen would always be an inspiration and a joy to him. But he was in no position at the present to even think of marriage. If ever a time came when he was both successful and wealthy, then there would be no hesitation on his part. But he was determined that Helen should have no half-promises to cling to, no talk of waiting for that time to come. She must feel free to continue their friendship or end it as she chose: be free to enjoy the company of other men—and if it were destined that way, to be able to marry another man if she wished.

So he held her close and kept a firm rein on the words which threatened to tumble from his lips. And Helen, crushed against him, yearned in vain for the comfort and reassurance which knowledge of his love would bring her . . .

CHAPTER TEN

It was six months since Isobel had told him that she meant to marry Frank Cummins. It was almost two months since he had been to the little white house. He knew they must wonder at his neglect but he could not bring himself to welcome the pain which such a visit would cause him.

He wondered if Isobel had set her wedding day but felt sure that either she or Lisa would have told him in a letter by this time. He heard frequently from Lisa: rarely from Isobel. It seemed to him that she was strangely reluctant to go ahead with her marriage to Frank Cummins. But Desmond had long since accepted her answer although he had not ceased to care for her. The very thought of her, a mental vision of her fair loveliness, could bring swift tumult to his blood, the sweet yet sad longing for her.

He could not rid himself of the certainty that Isobel returned his love, shared the same disturbing emotion. But her words had been definite enough and he could not believe her capable of lying. Why should she even want to lie? If she did indeed love him, there were no obstacles in their path.

He had accepted the inevitable for there was no point in fighting against her decision. But he could not help wondering at it. There had been between them a rare and remarkable affinity—a sweet and precious bond which was inexplicable but something to be treasured and treated with care. He had not denied it and neither had Isobel. Yet she had cast it aside as though it was of no importance—cast it aside in order to marry a man like Frank Cummins who was a pleasant enough fellow, to be sure, and no doubt had proved the value of his friendship many times. But it was a waste of Isobel's beauty and innocence and sensitivity for her to marry Frank. For her to become a farmer's wife seemed sacrilege.

He welcomed Lisa's letters for every now and again she would mention her sister—and these few words were water to a thirsty man. The letters were vital and interesting and emphasized Lisa's simplicity and intelligence. He had a great affection for Lisa—but it could never compare with the love he bore for Isobel. He sought some way, however, in which he could do something for Lisa—as he had searched for a way to help Michael and, indirectly, help Isobel. He would gladly give Isobel the world if she expressed a desire for it. But he was in no position to give her anything and he regretted this. There was always Lisa, though, who had had so little out of life—and he determined on a way to bring her happiness. He felt sure that his gesture would also earn Isobel's warm gratitude and give her pleasure, for he knew she was devoted to her sister. Her maternal solicitude for Lisa touched him very much yet he had a great sympathy for Isobel who had to take on responsibility and the burden of her brother and sister at such an early age. Yet it had done her no harm: the reverse if anything. She had matured quickly into a woman of quiet sweetness and charm and goodness. The purity of her soul shone from those lovely grey eyes.

He had formed a friendship with Ryan Nesbit very readily—for the man's sake as well as to please Helen who was so obviously in love with the artist. He had seen the few paintings which Ryan brought to the flat at his request and be had been struck by the man's talent and ability. He had seen him several times since that day and gradually found out more about him. His father had been a colonel: his mother the daughter of an Irish priest. At an early age, Ryan had left home, finding the sheltered surroundings of his home and family too restrictive. He had wandered from place to place, earning a few pounds here and there which had been sufficient for his simple needs. He had painted steadily, discarding his early work for the later and better work. On his father's death, he had found himself the possessor of a few hundred pounds and had immediately taken a boat to South Africa, He had lived roughly and simply and worked hard at his painting. He had sold a few canvases: had been taken up by a wealthy South African patron who fêted him for a few months until she tired of her protégé. Then Ryan had gone to Australia. He worked his way from one end of that big country to the other. His next action had been to return to Europe where he had lived for eighteen months, wandering like a nomad from country to country, selling an occasional painting, working in the fields and vineyards in order to eat. At last, he had returned to England—always his first love—and decided to settle down to an ordinary existence until he had enough money behind him to take up a nomad life once again. His travels, the open air and the hardy work had bronzed him and built his powerful physique. He had been in London a few weeks only when he met Helen Fairfax.

Ryan talked more easily to Desmond than he had ever done to Helen. The two men understood each other and there was a warm liking between them. He told Desmond of his sojourn in South Africa: his wealthy patron who had showered him with gifts and social introductions but expected a lover in return. He had refused and this had hastened her swift weariness of his charms. Ryan had hated her patronage and her social circle. He had developed a healthy hatred of wealthy socialites and their way of life. He had determined, when he left South Africa, that never again would he take such help from anyone, that he would remain independent in the future and discourage any friendship which arose between himself and a rich woman. This explained his first reluctance to continue the association with Helen—but he had fallen irrevocably in love with her even against his will and, once in love, he had found it impossible to forget her.

Desmond's first incredulous astonishment at the man's gift for art was easily explained by Ryan's confession that he had never attended any art school in his life. It was purely a natural gift which had expressed itself very early. He had soon realized that he was born to paint—so art came before any other consideration no matter at what cost to himself.

Desmond approved his independent spirit and made no attempt to discourage him from his office job. He understood the man's natural pride and determined to find a way to help him along the road to success without obviously undermining that pride.

It seemed that the solution to several problems came to him at one time. He was alone in his flat, a drink in his hand, cigarettes in the box beside him, a fire flickering in the hearth and the drapes drawn against the bitter cold of the evening.

He had been occupied with an article for a magazine but now he put it aside, took a cigarette and flicked a table lighter into life. He inhaled deeply and then let the blue-grey smoke trickle from his nostrils. The light from a standard lamp fell on his dark hair and threw a gentle illumination on his handsome features.

He thought again of Isobel. She was always in his thoughts and his love was unchanged. It grew stronger with every passing day. His lovely Isobel—but never to be his. A sigh escaped him and he ran his hand through the dark crisp waves of his hair—would he never be free of the torment and the longing. The future seemed bleak and empty and he realized only too well that he was no longer as self-sufficient as he had been in the past. He needed a woman in his life—and the woman he needed was Isobel. But as that was impossible, why did he not ask Lisa to share his life? She resembled Isobel strongly, both in looks and character. She had the same sweetness and purity of soul. She was innocent and lovely. He did not frame the words 'of fair and shining beauty' in his mind for they belonged forever to Isobel.

Sweet Lisa. He could find a modicum of happiness with her. It would be an unsatisfactory relationship for he was well aware that she could not hope to lead a normal married life. But he felt that he wanted no woman but Isobel—without her, he could easily live a celibate existence. Perhaps Isobel was delaying her marriage because Lisa must always be her first consideration, If he married Lisa, then Isobel would be free to take her happiness with Frank Cummins. He had taken the responsibility for Michael from her shoulders—why not Lisa, too? He could do so much for Lisa—and the prospect gave him pleasure. He knew she longed to travel extensively: very well, he could take her abroad. He knew she yearned for a more sophisticated life after the sheltered solitude she had always known: very well, they would live in London and she would meet all his friends; he would take her to the theatre, to art galleries, to night-clubs, to dinner parties. He enjoyed the social life. He would enjoy it even more when he was initiating Lisa into its pleasures. She was very young and must surely yearn to know more of life than she had already experienced: he was worldly and could teach her so many things. She would no doubt make him a good wife. She would never bore him because she had a vital intelligence and a swift enjoyment of life, an appealing vivacity. She was young and beautiful and naïve—he felt the need of a wife and if not Isobel, then surely her sister was an admirable choice.

He stubbed his cigarette and drained his glass. He rose to his feet and walked over to the fireplace, He bent down to place a fresh log on the fire and then kicked it into position. He felt relief and a certain contentment now that he had decided on a course of action. Foremost in his thoughts was the memory that Lisa loved him and would find happiness with him.

He called her to mind and was a little startled by the clarity of the vision. It had always been Isobel's image that preoccupied him and it was disturbing to find how easily he could visualize Lisa. Suddenly he thought of the miniature by her bedside—the enchanting infant with the apple—and he was filled with an ache of longing. He had analysed this now familiar ache and knew it to be his wish to have children of his own, But it would be impossible if he married Lisa. He sighed briefly. He would have to think of Michael as his son: he was a boy that any man would be proud to call son and Desmond had great faith in the man he would one day become.

But thinking of the miniature, another idea came to him. Ryan Nesbit had included a portrait among the canvases he showed to Desmond. It had shown remarkable talent and Ryan himself had said that it was among his best works. He would commission a portrait of Lisa. He was confident that Ryan would execute the commission with his usual care and attention to detail. When the portrait was finished, he would insist that Ryan submit it to the Royal Academy. If it were accepted, the man would be assured of notice and possibly success. There would be no question of having helped him in any way. It would be a business transaction in the first place and Desmond knew that he would want such a portrait of Lisa so that in years to come he could always remember how she had looked as a young woman. Once Ryan had captured the attention of the art critics and connoisseurs, he would no doubt receive many commissions which would bring him both wealth and fame. There would be nothing to prevent a marriage between him and Helen—and thus two more people of whom he was very fond would find happiness.

He grinned a little ruefully as he took another cigarette from the box. He felt somewhat like a benevolent god arranging lives to the benefit of the people concerned. Yet he could not bring about his own happiness. He would find contentment with Lisa and possibly peace of mind—always providing he could reconcile himself to life without Isobel and surely he had done that during these last months of longing and pain and futile desire, Now he could think of her marriage to Frank Cummins with a lessening of the pain and a sincere hope that she would find happiness.

He decided to contact Ryan Nesbit as soon as possible and broach the idea of Lisa's portrait. If he accepted the commission, and there was really no reason why he should refuse, then he would suggest a trip to the little white house so Ryan could study his subject. Helen could accompany them: he would like her to meet Isobel and Lisa and it would be the beginning of a friendship between the woman who had been his friend for many years and the woman who he was now determined to make his wife. Helen could be a great help to Lisa in the future, advising her on clothes and cosmetics, and perhaps passing on a little of her own sophistication. He would write to Isobel on the very next day and tell them of his intended visit. But he would not expect to stay at the house. The three of them could stay at an hotel in Hanleigh for the week-end.

At first, Ryan was a little suspicious when he spoke of the portrait to him. He turned from the window of Desmond's flat and studied him. Desmond had telephoned him and asked him to call in for an after-lunch drink. He had gone into the office that morning, and dispatched a few letters, talked to a new novelist whose first book they were publishing the next month, and then left with the information that he would not be in for a few days.

Now Ryan studied him closely. 'A portrait? I'm not sure that I like working to order, Desmond.'

Desmond grinned. 'Well, you'll have to

learn to like it for I've a feeling that in time your portraits are going to be in great demand, old chap. Have another drink?'

Ryan handed him his glass without demur. 'Who is this woman?'

'A very sweet and lovely girl of twenty-one,' Desmond replied, busying himself with the decanters. 'A great friend of mine. Quite possibly she will be my wife in a short time. Which explains why I'd like you to do the portrait. But you needn't give me an answer now, Ryan. I thought we'd run down for the week-end—then you can see Lisa for yourself and decide if you can do justice to her beauty.' He handed Ryan the fresh drink.

'Well, I'll consider it,' Ryan said at last, 'As long as this isn't a favour, Desmond?'

Desmond raised an eyebrow. 'A favour? Don't be ridiculous! I don't throw my money away unnecessarily, you know.'

'Why me?' Ryan demanded. 'There are dozens of portrait painters—names in the art world. You must know several of them. Why me?' he repeated.

'Because I've confidence in your work—and because I'd like to look at it in future years when your name is famous and synonymous with success and think to myself: well, this was the first of a long line of great portraits and I had a hand in its creation.' He grinned. 'Purely selfish, old chap. Quite seriously, Ryan, I shall be very grateful if you will do this for me. But give me your answer after you've seen Lisa.' He went on to talk about her, explained that she had been paralysed since birth but that no trace of bitterness tainted her soul. Quickly he gained Ryan's interest and sympathy and felt that half the battle was won.

Before he left, Ryan said: 'Where am I to paint this portrait—always providing I agree to do it,' he added quickly. 'If she's crippled, she won't be coming up to London—and I can only spare odd hours in the present circumstances.'

'Well, I rather thought you'd like to work down there—it's a lovely place, nice little house with the perfect atmosphere, in my opinion. Isobel and Lisa will make you very welcome, I know—and now that the boy is away at school, they've a spare bedroom. You'd have as much time as you liked—and when you didn't feel like working, well, there wouldn't be the need.'

'And my job?'

'I should throw it in, old chap. It's not really in your line, anyway. I'll give you a hundred pounds in advance on the portrait—always providing you agree to do it,' he added with a twinkle in his eyes. 'I think it will be one of the best things you've ever done—and should bring you in more commissions of a similar nature. You won't have to worry about an insurance office then.'

Ryan held out his hand. 'I never thought I'd

be accepting a helping hand from anyone again, Desmond, but oddly enough I don't resent it from you.' With these words, Desmond realized that he had not deceived the young man for an instant and he was grateful that Ryan accepted his help in the same spirit as it was offered.

They shook hands. 'You know, I'm only the spur,' Desmond told him, putting his other hand in a firm clasp on Ryan's shoulder. 'You don't really need any help from me or anyone. You're great enough to get where you're going on your own. But it might take years. At least try my way—it might not be successful but it doesn't pay to laugh at opportunities.'

That afternoon, he went to see Helen. He found her at home but preparing to go out to tea with a friend. She greeted him warmly.

'Hallo, my dear! Ryan telephoned me and told me of your commission. I think it's a wonderful idea—and how like you to think of it, You know, Desmond, you're the kindest man I know.'

'Well, I'm glad you like the idea. Ryan was more than a little dubious.'

'He's a strange man,' she said slowly. 'He seems to mistrust offers of help—but perhaps any offers he's had in the past have had a sting in their tail. Who knows? Would you like some coffee?'

'No, thanks. Did Ryan tell you about my plans for the week-end?'

'Yes. I should be furious with you for not including me—but I suppose the country at this time of the year isn't particularly attractive. I shall enjoy a lonely weekend and think of you two men in the snares of your women friends.'

'But I am including you,' he returned swiftly. 'I may not have said as much to Ryan—although I thought it was obvious—but I knew you would want to come with us. Anyway, I want you to come, Helen—I'm looking forward to having you meet my friends.'

He had mentioned them to her in the past and she had been intrigued by his interest in the two women who seemed to lead such a sheltered life deep in the heart of the country. When he told her that he was footing the bill for Michael Lomax's education, she had been even more intrigued, and it had surprised her a little that, at the busiest time of the year for him, he had taken time off to take the boy up to Scotland at the beginning of the school term. Her interest and sympathy had been stirred when he talked to her of their early bereavement of both parents, the natural acceptance of responsibility that Isobel had shouldered, the paralysis of the younger girl, and their attempts to earn a living by means of the little books for children.

'Well, that would be pleasant,' she admitted. 'I must confess that I'm curious about them. Tell me, darling, what charms do these two nun-like creatures have that they can lure you away from me?' She laughed up at him, her words light, yet there was possibly a trace of regret in her tone. She had long since realized that her love for Desmond had been a figment of an eager imagination. Now that she really loved, she knew there was no comparison between her emotion where Ryan was concerned and the old, familiar affection she had always known for Desmond.

'That you must see for yourself,' he retorted.

She glanced at him obliquely through her long lashes. Then a brief, hesitant pause. At last she said slowly: 'Ryan tells me that you spoke of marrying Lisa—the girl you want him to paint. True?'

'Possibly true.' He would not commit himself yet.

'If I had known you were still in the marriage market, I'd have waited longer before casting my eyes in Ryan's direction,' she assured him with a smile.

'Nonsense!' he said firmly. 'You and Ryan were made for each other.'

'Do you really think so?' she asked eagerly, her eyes alight with the warm glow he had come to recognize whenever she spoke of Ryan Nesbit.

'You're in love with him, aren't you?'

She nodded. 'Of course I am.'

'And he loves you?'

She looked down at her hands. 'Sometimes I'm sure of it—then other times I just don't know, Desmond. He's never committed himself.'

Desmond rose to his feet. 'Well, give him time, Helen. It isn't for me to say that he loves you—but I don't think there's much doubt about it. Give him time to do this portrait of Lisa—it will be a success, I'm sure of that. As soon as he feels that he has anything to offer you, he'll want to marry you.'

'Anything to offer me?' she cried with a trace of anguish. 'All I want is his love. He attaches too much importance to money and social position—I wish now that I'd never had either. If I'd been a typist or a shop assistant, Ryan and I would have been married by now, I suppose. But because I'm Helen Fairfax, socialite, his pride comes between us.'

'Never try to part a man from his pride, Helen,' Desmond cautioned her. 'Learn to live with it—as he has to. He doesn't like it any more than you do, I expect. Don't make things difficult for him. There, the sermon is ended—and I must go.'

'Wait—I'm going out. I'll come down with you. I'll just get my things.' She hurried from the room and returned in a few moments. She was striking and very beautiful. Desmond's glance carried admiration and affection and she smiled across the room at him, conscious of her own beauty and the effect it always had on men—yet always uncaring now unless it were the man she loved.

CHAPTER ELEVEN

Frank tamped his pipe carefully and slowly. He glanced up at Isobel as she stood by the table, arranging flowers in a deep bowl. He studied her fair head with its short curls, the slim curve of her arched neck as she bent over her task. He opened his mouth to speak then closed it firmly and did not the break the silence which had been in the room for the last few minutes.

Isobel sensed that something was on his mind: she had known it when he arrived. He had greeted her in his usual, kindly manner but with a look in his eyes which had disturbed her because she could not define its cause. Now she waited for him to speak, Lisa was already in bed for she had a slight cold and a bad headache.

Michael was now away at school and from his letters, neatly and pedantically written, Isobel and Lisa gathered that he found that it came up to all his expectations. But the little white house missed his presence. There was a feeling of emptiness without him and there were times when Isobel wondered if she had been right to let him go away from her care and affection. But she could not doubt his present happiness and he had made several friends. She had been dubious about the long journey but Desmond Crane had written to assure her that he would meet Michael at the London terminus if she put him on the train. She was unable to leave Lisa to take him up to London so, reluctantly, she had to let him travel alone. But Desmond had promised to take him up to Scotland to the new school from London. He regretted that an important appointment prevented him from collecting Michael at his home . . .

It was several weeks since they had seen Desmond. Isobel wondered if his continued absence was deliberate. She missed him with a constant sense of loss and the dull heartache which her rejection of his love had brought her. She remembered vividly the expression of bewilderment and hurt in his eyes when she told him of her intention to marry Frank: she recalled her own determination to sacrifice her own emotions in Lisa's interest. But now she wondered if her sacrifice had been in vain for Desmond had not turned to Lisa, as she had hoped. He had sent her several small gifts and she had recognized his handwriting on letters which came for Lisa. But he made no attempt to visit them and she knew his neglect had hurt and dismayed her sister as well as herself. But there seemed no way in which either of them could change matters. Desmond was apparently staying away because he cared for

Isobel and because he knew that Lisa was in love with him.

Lost in her own thoughts, she turned with a start when Frank finally spoke. 'That chap from London hasn't been down to see you for some time, Isobel, I guess whatever it was he needed, he found you didn't supply it, after all.' His pipe was well alight now and he looked comfortable in the shabby old armchair. But his tone was a little strained and Isobel had the swift impression that he had meant to say something entirely different and changed his mind at the last moment.

She replied easily, 'I expect he's busy, Frank. I've heard from him once or twice. I thought it was very kind of him to take Michael up to Scotland. I couldn't leave Lisa and it was a long way for him to travel alone when he's never left us before.'

'Aye, he seems a kind enough man,' Frank agreed. 'I'm surprised you agreed to let him pay Michael's fees at that posh school, though. A complete stranger taking over your responsibilities—I must say it puzzles me. Not that it's any of my business.'

'We couldn't afford to send him and it would be a great pity to let his good brain go to waste. A good education will mean a good career later on, Frank—it worried me quite a lot wondering what he would do when he left the village school.'

'He has a liking for the land. He could have

164

come to work on the farm with me. In time, I'd have bought him a few acres—or rented them—and he could have set up on his own account. He'd make a good farmer.'

Isobel sat down opposite him and picked up some sewing. 'Yes, I know, Frank. We've discussed that before—but when the opportunity came along, I didn't think it was right to deny him the chance of a better education than the village school can offer. It's quite possible he'll want to farm when he's left school—but the education will still be useful.'

There was a brief pause, then, as though he had suddenly plucked up courage, Frank said abruptly: 'I came over tonight to tell you that I'm getting married, Isobel.'

She stared at him in some surprise. It was an unexpected piece of news. Although he had never spoken of his feelings, she had always been sure that he cared for her and hoped to marry her. 'Married?' she repeated.

'Yes. I'm marrying Ella—Bill Hodge's youngest. We've fixed the date for next month. There doesn't seem anything to wait for and the farm's doing well. Bill is downright pleased about the match. Ella's a farmer's daughter and she's lived on a farm all her life. She's a nice little thing and I guess we'll get along pretty well together.' He had turned a deep brick-red and she fully understood his embarrassment. He knew well enough that she had always taken his feelings for granted. He knew too that she was taken aback at his news.

'Why, I'm very pleased, Frank,' she managed to say at last. 'Ella is a nice girl and I should think she'll make you a good wife.'

He said hastily, still embarrassed, 'It's a bit of a shock to you, Isobel. I've always had you in mind as my wife—but lately . . . well, to be quite honest, I've realized you don't love me and wouldn't want to marry me. I'm well over thirty and I'd like to have a son who'll carry on the farm. I hoped that in time you would feel about me as I've always felt about you. But I'm not blind and I saw how you reacted to that London chap. I knew I could never make you feel like that about me—so I stopped hoping and looked around for someone else to marry.'

Isobel's sewing lay idle in her lap. She met his eyes squarely. 'I'm sorry, Frank. I'm very fond of you—I always have been—but I don't think I would ever have married you. I had made up my mind to do so, if you ever got around to asking me, but of course I know now that it wouldn't have been the right thing to do.'

'You're in love with Crane,' he said quietly. 'When he stopped coming here, I told myself that either you had made it obvious and he wasn't interested—or else that he was interested and you wouldn't marry him because of Lisa. Then I thought I would ask you as soon as I could—but I just couldn't bring myself to do it. I was afraid you might

166

say yes—and I don't want to marry any woman who loves someone else.'

'It's never a very good idea,' she agreed quietly. 'It would have been very wrong of me to marry you loving Desmond—for, of course, you're right. I do love him and he was interested. But I couldn't hurt Lisa—and I'm still hoping that one day he will love her and not me.'

Frank shook his head slowly. 'No one can love to order, lass. I can understand how you feel about Lisa, but you're entitled to your happiness—and opportunity only knocks once—or so we're told.'

'Are you in love with Ella?' she asked, a little shyly.

'I wouldn't say love,' he replied at last. He chose his words carefully. 'I'm very fond of her—very fond. I've only ever loved one woman in my life, Isobel, and that's you . . .'

She interrupted him. 'Is it fair to marry Ella when you don't love her? It will be a living lie, Frank!'

He shook his head again. 'I've thought about it a lot. It's worried me, the fairness of it. But it came about suddenly, you see—I can't remember that I even asked her to marry me. But she loves me—and I suppose I said something careless-like and she took me up on it quickly. She rushed to tell her father we were getting married and he was delighted— kept pumping my hand up and down and telling me he'd always hoped to have me as a son-in-law. Well, I didn't see how I could get out of it then—let alone disappoint Ella.' He added diffidently, 'You see, she's no slip of a girl although she's pretty enough to pass as one. She's about a year younger than me and it's high time she married. There aren't many men in these parts without a wife—and as I said, she's in love with me.'

Isobel rose and crossed to his side. She brushed back a lock of his hair and pressed her lips to his forehead. 'How kind you are, Frank. Much too kind—and you see where kindness leads you!'

He grinned. 'This was a few weeks ago. I've grown used to the idea now, I guess. I rather like it and I'm looking forward to marrying Ella. Some people would say we're of a kind— well-suited. But you, Isobel—well, you're different to the women around here. Better class, I suppose. You come from a good family—and I'm only a farmer. The reason I never asked you to marry me was because I always thought you were too far above me—it seemed too presumptuous on my part. Your father being Nigel Lomax and all. I was born to marry Ella Hodges. You were born to marry some chap like Crane. That's how it seems to me, anyway.'

'Oh, Frank!' She was touched by his gentle humility. Suddenly sadness engulfed her. 'How cruel life can be sometimes, Frank. I should

168

love you—but I don't. I'm in love with a man I shall never be able to marry because Lisa loves him too and she must come first. She's had so much unkindness from life. You're in love with me yet if you married me you wouldn't be happy. Ella loves you—but you can't love her . . .' She broke off.

'But I'm going to marry her,' he said firmly. 'And I don't intend to have any regrets. If you take my advice, Isobel—which you won't— you'll seek out Crane and put your life to rights. Lisa wouldn't thank you for giving him up for her sake. As for the unkindness she's had from life, she's a happier person than most, my dear, and she counts her blessings.' He got up and stretched his tall body. 'Ah well, I must go home to my bed and let you get to yours. Isobel. You'll come to the wedding, you and Lisa?'

She nodded. 'Of course we'll come—and I hope you'll be happy, Frank. I wish things could have been different.'

He put an arm about her shoulders and hugged her. 'No, 'tis better as they are, Isobel. It isn't for us to wonder at the workings of Fate, after all. Lisa knows all about acceptance—learn a few lessons from her. I have.'

When he had gone, Isobel curled up on the settee with her thoughts which were very confused for everything that Frank had said had disturbed her. It had come as a shock to know that the faithful friend who had always loved her was going to marry Ella Hodges. But she understood his point of view and she had been truthful when she told him that she would have refused if he had offered her marriage. It was all very well to tell herself that she would make him a good wife and ensure that he never regretted it, even though she loved Desmond. But putting good intentions into practice was a different matter. Fond as she was of Frank, marriage with him was as unthinkable now as it had ever been. But it was a little disconcerting to find that he had calmly looked around for another wife and found one, all in a few weeks. But she wished him every happiness and only longed for a little of it herself. Tears of longing and self-pity engulfed her and she buried her face in a cushion. After a few minutes, she pulled herself together and sat up, sternly admonishing herself not to be a fool, that she had chosen her own sadness for Lisa's sake, and that it was up to her to do something to ensure her sister's happiness. Perhaps she should write to Desmond and invite him down for a week-end. Then do all in her power to throw him and Lisa together. There must be some way to bring about a marriage between them.

Frank's almost-forgotten remarks on the subject of marriage between a healthy man like Desmond Crane and an invalid Lisa

170

suddenly came back to her. It was scarcely fair to press a marriage between them. Lisa could never be a normal wife to any man. Children were out of the question. But she could love as intensely as any woman and surely she was entitled to her share of happiness? Desmond was kind and understanding and considerate. He would not expect too much of Lisa—if only he loved her and not Isobel. Lisa had far more worthwhile qualities than her sister: she could make Desmond a good wife in other ways . . .

So Isobel argued with herself and before she went to bed that night, she sat at the table in the small sitting-room and wrote to Desmond, chiding him in a friendly manner for not having been to see them for so many weeks, assuring him that they heard from Michael frequently and he was very happy, and finally inviting him to come down for the week-end if he had no other engagement. She read it over and before she could change her mind, hastily put it in an envelope, sealed and addressed it, and hurried down the lane to the postbox which served the few farms in the district surrounding the village.

Slowly, she walked back to the little white house which stood out sharply in the bright moonlight . . .

She received his reply two days later. It was brief but friendly and told her that he was arriving on Friday evening with a couple of friends. She was not to concern herself about accommodation—they would be staying at Hanleigh for the week-end. He had been coming down to see her that week-end, anyway, but the invitation had pleased him.

Lisa studied her face. 'Well, what does he say? Is he coming?' she asked anxiously, for Isobel had told her of the letter of invitation. Her sister had broken the news to her of Frank's wedding and Lisa had replied: 'Well, what did you expect? It wasn't likely that he would wait for ever for some encouragement from you, Isobel—I'm glad he's getting married to Ella. Dear old Frank—he deserves to be happy if only because of the years of kindness and friendship his given us.' Now she repeated again, 'Is he coming, Isobel?'

Isobel folded the letter. 'Yes. He's staying at Hanleigh for the week-end but he'll be here to see us on Friday evening. He's bringing some friends with him.'

'Does he say who they are?'

Isobel handed her the letter. 'Read it for yourself. He just says "a couple of friends".' She went back to the reading of the proof of their latest little book.

Both girls talked over the coming week-end. They were intrigued by the mention of Desmond's friends and were openly a little disappointed that they were not to have his sole attention.

'It doesn't sound as though we'll see much of him if he's staying at Hanleigh,' Lisa

172

commented. 'His friends will probably take up most of his time in other ways.'

'Maybe he particularly wants us to meet them.'

'I suppose they're men,' Lisa said idly.

'They could be women,' Isobel reminded her. 'We mustn't suppose that he hasn't women friends, Lisa—after all, he's a very handsome man.'

'Yes.' Her sister agreed and something that was almost a sigh escaped her. 'I wonder why he hasn't been to see us for some time, Isobel?'

'I expect he's been busy.' She gave the same answer she had given Frank.

'Will you wash my hair tonight? I'd like to look nice for the week-end. I wish I had a new dress—I'm sure I shall look terribly dowdy after the London women Desmond knows.'

'Lisa, you always look nice. Besides, Desmond comes here to get away from those London women, I imagine.' After a brief pause, she added diffidently, 'Are you still fond of him, Lisa?'

Lisa did not answer directly. Isobel glanced at her sister and found her eyes tinged with sadness while a faint trace of colour stained her cheeks. Then Lisa said slowly, 'Yes. I've missed him these last weeks. It will be nice to see him again.'

There was a hint of sternness in Isobel's tone, 'That isn't what I meant. You told me once that you loved him. Do you still?'

Isobel had never told her sister the true explanation of the marked poem. She had never confided the conversation she had had with Desmond and her impulsive reply that she was going to marry Frank. She often felt that she should disillusion Lisa, for despite the question she knew that her sister still cared for Desmond Crane, but she found it impossible. How could she take away any of Lisa's happiness, she asked herself, remembering Lisa's certainty that Desmond loved in return. She had been dealt enough blows in life—another of such nature would surely break her heart. Even her sweet, natural acceptance of all things could not withstand such knowledge surely.

Lisa looked into Isobel's face. She had never lied to Isobel in her life and she had no intention of lying now. 'Yes, I do love him. But I'm quite reconciled to the fact that he doesn't love me. I knew it when he last came here. He was dismayed to find that I cared . . .'

'You told him?' Isobel asked swiftly, bewildered.

'Not in as many words. But he knew.' She sighed. 'How could I pretend, Isobel? It was in my eyes and in my happiness. When he kissed me he tasted it on my lips. Desmond is no fool—and he certainly isn't blind. He knew, Isobel—and he was unhappy about it. I think that's why we haven't seen him lately. Perhaps

174

he hoped I would get over him if I didn't see him for a while.' She smiled with tenderness. 'I'm not the kind of woman who falls in and out of love easily. Once I love it's for ever. That's how it is with Desmond. But, darling, I'm not unhappy about it—just a little sad sometimes when I think of the happiness I could have known if Desmond loved me too. But I always knew I would never marry.' She smiled again. 'It wouldn't be fair to any man, Isobel, to saddle him with a wife like me.'

'Give him time,' Isobel said though tears almost choked her and tightened her throat. 'I know he's fond of you—in time he'll come to love you. Don't give up now, Lisa.' She came to kneel by Lisa's wheelchair and took her hands. 'I'd give anything to see you happy, darling. I know Desmond could make you happy. If there is anything I can do, I will do it.'

Lisa released one of her hands and stroked Isobel's fair hair. 'Do you remember that poem, Isobel? *"Of fair and shining beauty"*. Do you know that it could apply to you just as much as to me? I've often thought that Desmond possibly meant it for you.'

'No, no, he didn't,' Isobel rejected her sister's words vehemently. 'He sent the book to you. He must have meant it for you.'

'I think Desmond loves you.'

Isobel shook her head. 'That's nonsense! Anyway, I don't want him to care for me. I'd

175

much rather that he loved and married you.'

Lisa looked down at her fair head. 'You really mean that too.' She smiled with a trace of humour. 'You should have been a knight in days of old—or a cavalier, Isobel. Bold and chivalrous, noble and loyal. I wonder if I could be so unselfish? I don't think so. If I loved a man and knew that he loved me in return, I'd never give up my happiness—no, not for anyone. Not even for you, Isobel, and I love you very much.'

Isobel rose to her feet. 'You're talking nonsense,' she said again. 'I'm no Joan of Arc. I'm not in love with Desmond and he thinks of me only as a friend. So I'm not being either noble or unselfish. I'm going to put the kettle on—a cup of tea should cure us both of these fantasies.' With that she walked out of the room. Lisa looked after her and her lips were smiling though her eyes were still sad. A tear squeezed through her lashes and trickled slowly down the curve of her cheek. When she tasted it salt on her lips, she brushed her eyes with the back of her hand and admonished herself sternly that there was nothing to cry about: she had made up her mind. It was terribly apparent that Isobel did love Desmond: it was just as obvious that he loved her. The emotion which they shared seemed to touch them both with a bright radiance and when they were together the rare and precious bond between them seemed to Lisa to

176

represent itself as a beam of light, rich and golden, which linked their two spirits. There was no place for Lisa in Desmond's life. Though he might sense her love, it must remain unspoken. She would be content to rejoice in the knowledge of their mutual happiness.

CHAPTER TWELVE

IT was no sports car this time that drove down the narrow lane but a big black saloon. It was a bitter November evening and Helen was wrapped in furs as she sat with Ryan's comforting arm about her shoulders. They had settled in at the hotel in Hanleigh, enjoyed an excellent dinner and were now arriving at the little white house,

The trees now were gaunt and barren, stark against the greyness of the sky—a grey so sombre as to be almost night. The white house was sharply etched in their sight and looked a little forlorn without the splendour of the verdant lawn and bright flowers.

As Desmond pushed open the gate, he again knew the now familiar sensation of homecoming and his heart lifted. He turned to his friends with a warm smile that was almost a welcome to this haven of peace and contentment. With his hand under Helen's elbow and Ryan one step behind, they walked towards the door. He was surprised that Isobel was not already there to greet them for she must surely have heard the car. He raised his hand to the knocker but before he could lift it, the door opened and Isobel stood there. He looked down at her and felt a momentary fear that they were unwelcome. Her lovely face lacked its usual radiance and he caught a glimpse of haunting sadness in her grey eyes. It was gone in a moment as she smiled.

He introduced his friends and she was composed and serene and welcoming. They all went into the small sitting-room where Lisa sat by the bright fire, an eager, expectant expression on the sweet face which was turned to them. Desmond heard Ryan catch his breath slightly and his smile widened at the reaction to Lisa's innocent loveliness,

Helen threw Desmond a quick, almost reproachful glance—and he knew that she wished he had spoken more of the two women who lived in the little white house and seemed to permeate the atmosphere with their own quiet peace and beauty.

Within a few minutes, the introductions were completed and Helen had thrown off her furs and was sitting near Lisa by the fire, talking easily and warmly to the girl. Ryan was wandering about the room, studying the paintings which were the work of Nigel Lomax—an artist he had always admired and

178

appreciated, His hands thrust in his pockets, a cigarette between his lips, his springy brown hair rumpled, he was perfectly at his ease. Isobel excused herself from the room and a moment later, Desmond slipped away. He found her in the kitchen, the kettle on for coffee, and she was laying cups and saucers on a tray. She looked up as he entered. She was startled by his sudden entry for her thoughts had been as busy as her hands.

Hearing the car engine, Isobel had hurried to the window as Lisa demanded: 'Do you think that's Desmond? He's very late.'

Unobserved, Isobel watched Desmond as he got out of the car and stood looking at the house for one long moment. Then he had turned back and helped Helen Fairfax to step down from the car. Isobel had noted Helen's expression as she looked up at Desmond and spoke, laughter touching her lips and eyes. The words did not reach Isobel. Desmond had inclined his head a little towards Helen and his smile had been brilliant, rich, holding a trace of contentment—it had been a happy smile which embraced the woman by his side and swift suspicion had thrust its stab into Isobel's heart. Helen was more than beautiful: elegant and poised, tall and slender and raven-haired.

Isobel had taken very little notice of the tall, powerful young man who stepped into the lane after Helen. Her eyes were on Desmond as he pushed open the gate: as he walked along the path beside Helen, a solicitous hand at her elbow, that smile still lingering as she talked to him.

She had been very conscious of Helen's charm as Desmond introduced her and the two women greeted each other, conventionally, but with the age-old hostility sparking in their eyes for a brief second as each regarded the other. Two women: both lovely; both interested in the same man—or that was how it seemed to Isobel.

These had been her thoughts as she moved about the kitchen with her deft movements. She dwelt in her mind on the hint of possessiveness in Helen's manner as she walked beside Desmond down the path and as she turned to him on their entry into the sitting-room. Her words still ran in Isobel's ears. *'Darling, no wonder you couldn't find the words to describe this place. It's lovely—so peaceful!'* Then, lowering her voice, *'She's delightful—no wonder I felt a little jealous—all is explained now!'* She had lowered her voice yet Isobel had heard the words. It was not difficult to put a swift construction on them.

Sadness had filled her being—and at the earliest opportunity Isobel had slipped from the room. Sadness still haunted her—that and a sense of loss mingled with the knowledge that she had brought all this upon herself. She and Desmond had known an instinctive communion of the spirit: they had been drawn together by something beyond their control; they had known a promise of rare and wonderful happiness—but Isobel, afraid of the stirrings of emotion and fearful for Lisa's vulnerability, had denied all these things and hastily prevented Desmond from speaking of them.

If he had found consolation elsewhere—and it certainly seemed that way—then she could not blame him. She had not offered him any hope, any light, any happiness. She had gently but firmly closed one door to him and expected him to open another. He had—but it had not been the expected door. Instead of turning to Lisa, as she had hoped, he had chosen his own woman.

She remembered Frank's words: *'No one can love to order, lass'*. Well, she had not ordered Desmond to love Lisa but she must have made her hopes very clear during the past months. She had thrown them together as often as possible: left them alone in the hope that her movements were subtle; encouraged Desmond to talk of Lisa and introduced the subject many times herself. Certainly he had understood her motives and this was the reason for his long absence from them. He had found Isobel lacking in sensitivity, had misunderstood her motives, had been disappointed in them both—or perhaps knowing he could never love Lisa, he had preferred not to hurt her by his frequent

181

presence at the house.

But surely he knew that Lisa would be hurt by the presence of Helen? And not only Lisa, her heart cried—not only Lisa!

Now, as he stood with his back against the closed door, she looked up at him. He leaned his head back and shut his eyes for a brief moment. Then he opened them and smiled at her.

'It's wonderful to be here again,' he said quietly. 'I miss the place so much when I'm away from it.' He grinned suddenly. 'If I had the right, I'd be here all the time—you'd be thoroughly fed up with me, Isobel.'

'And the office?' she asked lightly.

'Oh, that could go hang,' he retorted. He drew out his cigarette-case and inserted a cigarette between his lips. He fumbled in his pocket for a lighter but Isobel lit a match from the gas ring and held it up to him. He bent his head over the flame. When the cigarette was well alight, he exhaled blue-grey smoke and murmured his thanks. 'How's Michael? Have you heard from him lately?'

She nodded. 'I had a letter this week. He's fine—looking forward to the Christmas holidays, of course.'

'Yes, they're almost upon us, aren't they? I'll make a note of the date later—I shall enjoy running up to Scotland to collect him.' His voice took on a faintly nostalgic tone. 'You know, when I took him up to the school, all the old memories came flooding back. The place has hardly altered at all through the years—and I was jolly pleased to see a couple of my old masters still going strong. Of course, they were very young when I was there—and they've aged a good deal.'

A smile flickered at Isobel's lips at the sound of that word 'jolly'. But it was gone in an instant, chased away by a sobering thought. She said slowly, lifting the kettle from the gas stove as it boiled, 'I hope you never regret taking on Michael's school fees. He's very happy there—and it would be a terrible blow to him if we ever had to take him away.'

Desmond frowned. 'I can't visualize such a necessity ever arising, Isobel. Why should I regret it?'

Isobel could not mention the fears in her heart that he meant to marry Helen Fairfax: that one day he might have a son of his own who would need education and who would take all the school fees he could afford; that Helen might resent his generous action on Michael's behalf and insist that the boy was not his responsibility. So she said vaguely, 'Oh, I don't know. One never knows what might happen.'

He took the loaded tray from her and she opened the kitchen door for him. 'Just a minute, Isobel,' he said quickly. She looked at him in swift inquiry. 'I don't want you to speak of this to Lisa yet, but I'm hoping that Ryan will paint her portrait for me. He's a talented artist and I'm backing him to become a successful one. I brought him here this weekend so he could get to know Lisa and decide whether he wants to take on the job I've offered. If he does, you'll let him stay here for a while, won't you? I thought he could have Michael's bedroom when the boy's at school—and perhaps manage on the sofa during the holidays if he wants to start on the portrait right away. Your father found that this place was the perfect setting for his work. He worked well and happily here. Ryan will no doubt sense the same atmosphere. Will you have him, Isobel?'

She had listened to this recital without a sign of interruption. When he stopped speaking there was a moment's hesitation. Then she said, 'Perhaps we'd better wait and see if he wants to paint the portrait, Desmond.'

'With Lisa as his subject, he'd be crazy to refuse,' he said quickly. 'She'll make a wonderful model—and I know Ryan has the ability to capture her innocence and purity of expression.' He added, scanning her face, 'What's the matter? Don't you like Ryan?'

She laughed lightly. 'After five minutes, yes. I think he's rather nice—he's very young, isn't he? But he may not be so keen on staying here, Desmond—he might prefer the village pub. After all, he could get terribly bored with his subject if he lives in the same house as Lisa all the time.'

'I doubt that very much. I've never been bored by Lisa yet—and believe me, my dear, I'm far more demanding than that young man.'

'This coffee will be getting cold,' Isobel said in reply. 'I hope Lisa's coping with our guests by herself,' she added lightly.

The simple way she had used the word 'our' touched him. He did not doubt that she had included him in that little word rather than as one of the guests. He said impulsively, 'You're very sweet, Isobel.'

The colour rushed to stain her cheeks, almost to the roots of her hair. Without a word, she walked on and pushed open the sitting-room door and Desmond followed her.

The evening passed pleasantly.

Isobel tried to quench the tide of resentment as she talked to Helen. She could not help liking the woman. She seemed singularly unaffected and her charm was hard to resist. She was open in her admiration for the simple, almost shabbily furnished room: she passed a few knowledgeable remarks about Nigel Lomax's paintings; she was kind to Lisa without a hint of pity or patronage in her manner. There was no more of the possessiveness in her attitude to Desmond. Indeed, she shared her favours equally between the two men. Desmond seemed to be in good mood, light-hearted, full of easy

185

conversation, attentive and affectionate with Lisa, proud and yet modest about his own kind generosity when he spoke of Michael. Lisa, open-hearted and impulsive Lisa, had taken readily to Desmond's friends. She was flushed with excitement: her wit was sparkling and intelligent; she seemed to gain fresh confidence with every passing moment. Isobel was mostly quiet, letting the conversation and laughter flow over her, only occasionally inserting a remark of her own; a smile touched her lips for she was happy to see Lisa's pleasure in the evening, and though Desmond's advent had also brought her sadness, it also brought joy that he should be once again at the little house, so near to her. She could listen to the even, rich quality of his voice, study the handsome, mobile features, smile across the room into his dark, glowing eyes, feel the security and happiness of his presence.

Desmond found it was an effort to concentrate on the light conversation. He was too conscious of Isobel's quiet figure opposite him, the firelight flickering in her eyes and on her fair skin, reflecting in the rich glow of her scarlet dress. Their eyes met occasionally and she would smile—her warm, sweet smile with its quality of friendship and affection. He resented the presence of the others. He longed for the quiet solitude that he had known in this room when he sat before the fire with Isobel

186

and his hand was on her short, fair curls. With a vivid memory that brought him pain, he felt again her slender hands on his head, drawing his face down to her; knew again the light brushing of her lips against his and the sweet perfume of her hair. Once more he suffered the anguish which she had brought him by her light-spoken words: *'I'm going to marry Frank . . .'* Yet she had not married him. There was no ring sparkling on her left hand. She had not made one mention of the man. Lisa had not spoken of him either. The thought of Lisa reminded him of his decision and he lost the thread of the conversation in that moment. He had made up his mind to marry Lisa. He looked across at her now and studied the animated face as she listened to Ryan's interesting account of his life in South Africa. She was really alive and vital. The cloud of silken hair fell about her face to her shoulders. It was pure gold in the soft lighting—framing her face with an aureole of light. Something twisted inside him and his throat ached for her vulnerability. Was he right to make her his wife? She was too sensitive to be deceived. He knew that he could never pretend to a love for her—and yet could he bring himself to offer marriage to Lisa without love. Was it fair to her youthful dreams? Would he not in time destroy the love which he knew she cherished for him—because he could not return that love? Love could not live without response—

yet while that thought came to him, he refuted it, knowing the emotion for Isobel which held him captive grew stronger with every passing day despite its lack of encouragement or response. Deep in his heart the swift certainty that his love did indeed find a response in Isobel's being leapt to life and refused to be quenched. He glanced at Isobel—but her eyes were turned to the leaping flames of the fire and the lines of her face, illuminated by firelight and lamplight, were sad and spoke of loneliness. Once more he cursed the presence of Lisa and his friends, longed to take Isobel into his arms and kiss away the sadness, smooth away the loneliness with the comfort which only he could offer with faith in its welcome.

But if she had given her promise to Frank Cummins, then she would not break her word. Isobel was that kind of person—and Desmond knew she would not appreciate any persuasion on his part. If he could persuade her to break the promise—which he doubted—she would always know a fleeting sadness that she had hurt Frank and in her heart would be anger against herself and against Desmond too. He could not risk this. It was better to leave things as they were: better to marry Lisa, as he had decided, and give Isobel her freedom to follow the star she had chosen. A tiny sigh escaped him. His star was unattainable: the brightest star in his heavens—pure gold and unspeakably lovely—but out of his reach. He could follow his star for ever but would never know its warmth, would always gaze upon it from afar . . .

He knew that before the week-end was over he would have to talk to Isobel. If he could drive over alone from Hanleigh and ask to speak to her, then he would tell her that he hoped one day to make Lisa his wife—as soon as Lisa herself had grown used to the idea. He would ask Isobel to pave the way for him, remembering Lisa's innocence and inherent shyness. If necessary, he would let Isobel believe that he loved her sister—for she might not consent to marriage between them unless there was mutual love.

Perhaps he could assume an emotion he did not feel—but here doubt assailed him. How could be lie to the woman he loved? As she had found it impossible to lie to him. No, Isobel would have to know the truth but he would persuade her that it was the best thing for all concerned. Lisa would find happiness; he would know a modicum of contentment; Isobel would be free to marry Frank Cummins. She must agree to his suggestion—and he felt sure that she would, if only to ensure her sister's happiness.

He was very quiet as they drove back to Hanleigh. Ryan and Helen respected his silence for they had plenty to fill their thoughts.

Helen had liked the house and its occupants. She had felt a stirring of impulsive affection for the young Lisa and Isobel's quiet strength of character had intrigued her.

But she was puzzled. Desmond had said that he hoped to marry Lisa: surely pity did not prompt him to such an action? She knew him too well and she was sensitive to the bond which existed between Desmond and Isobel. They had exchanged nothing but casual conversation yet Helen had noticed that Desmond slipped from the room to have a few moments alone with Isobel and she had noticed too the flush which ruffled the woman's composure when she preceded him into the room when they returned with the coffee. What had Desmond said to her to bring about the rush of hot blood to her cheeks? Why that air of haunting sadness? Why Desmond's quiet scrutiny of Isobel which he had thought went unobserved—and Helen had sensed his impatience and restlessness. She remembered the indefinable difference in him since he had met Isobel and Lisa: he had told her of his sojourn at the cottage and his chance meeting with the two women on his way back to London. Now Helen put two and two together—and she was convinced that it was Isobel and not Lisa who had brought about that difference in him. Yet he intended to marry Lisa. She had no answer to the enigma. There seemed no reason why he should not be free to love Isobel and know her response. A woman in love herself Helen recognized the emotion in other women. Yes: Isobel loved Desmond—but so did Lisa. Was it this knowledge mingled with affectionate pity that prompted Desmond to offer Lisa marriage rather than her sister? That was no basis for marriage—and she could not visualize a man like Desmond Crane marrying a woman who would never be able to live a normal life. He was normal and healthy with all the natural instincts of a man—was he really prepared to forego his own feelings for Isobel and his natural desires for a normal marriage which would bring the blessings of children? If so, why? Helen wished she knew the answer.

Ryan's thoughts were filled with Lisa. He knew that he would accept Desmond's commission. He knew the urge to paint, to capture that beauty on canvas, to create a rare and sensitive image of her loveliness. His arm tightened about Helen's shoulders with his thoughts. He felt in himself a new confidence—he would do justice to Desmond's hopes and to Lisa's sweet fairness. He would know both success and riches in time—and then he would ask Helen to marry him. For he loved her with every part of his artist's being and he could not visualize his life without her. She was his inspiration and his love. He was impatient to begin work on the portrait. He looked forward to a long sojourn in that little white house where an artist so much greater than he could ever be had lived and worked and known fulfilment and happiness.

Not only admiration for Lisa's beauty but also a great admiration for her simplicity and the purity which shone from her eyes filled his being. She was unlike any woman he had ever met and he felt it would be a privilege to live in the same house with her and get to know her true and complete worth. He was grateful to Desmond for the opportunity, not only of cherishing the friendship which had already sprung into being, but of wielding his paintbrush to his heart's content. Here was the freedom and the unlimited time he had longed for since he arrived back in England—and Desmond Crane had made it possible. He would leave behind the cramping life in an insurance office and shake off the dust of city streets and feel himself his own man again.

There was no hesitation in him when later that night Desmond asked him if he had made that decision.

Ryan said quickly, his eyes shining, 'I'll gladly paint Lisa's portrait for you. I appreciate very much what you're offering me, Desmond—I can never repay you in full. The very least I can do is to refuse payment of any kind for the portrait.'

Desmond shook his head. 'I'd rather we kept this on a business basis, Ryan. You will

192

thank me for it in time—knowing that only your genius brought you success and not philanthropy on my part. You'll need money, anyway—I don't suppose you've managed to save very much these last few months. I think Isobel will be willing for you to stay at the house—but we mustn't let you be an extra burden for her. I suggested making you an advance of a hundred pounds—let's agree on that, old chap.'

The following morning, he told Helen that he was driving over to see Isobel on a private matter. She nodded and added impulsively: 'Does that mean you've changed your mind, Desmond?'

He raised an eyebrow. 'About what?'

'Marrying Lisa, of course—I think it would be very foolish of you.'

His face took on a guarded expression. He took up his spoon and began to stir his coffee slowly, absently. 'If I don't marry Lisa, I shall never marry anyone. And lately I'm beginning to feel the need of a wife, a real home and family of my own.' As soon as the words were uttered he realized his mistake.

Helen leaped into the opening. 'That's why you'd be foolish—it might not be impossible for Lisa to have a child but I would imagine it to be extremely unwise. You may be very fond of her and she seems to be devoted to you, Desmond—but how long can a marriage be happy on such a basis? In time you will probably bore and irritate each other. She seems a very intelligent young woman—she is probably as aware as I am that Isobel is the one you love. Do you really think she'll accept your proposal on those terms? Can you imagine Lisa hurting her sister in such a way?'

Desmond looked up quickly. 'Am I so transparent?'

'I know you very well,' she reminded him gently.

Their eyes held for a long moment. Then Desmond said with a world of resignation in his tone, 'Isobel has already promised to marry someone else. I have no right to love her—but it's something that no man can fight against when it's a love as powerful as mine for Isobel,'

Swift sympathy sped to Helen's eyes. 'Oh, my dear—I had no idea! I'm sorry.' Did this explain Isobel's sadness, she wondered—was the woman aware that Desmond loved her and regretted that she had to hurt him? She added impulsively and without thought: 'So you'll marry one sister because you can't have the other?'

Desmond frowned. 'I suppose that's true—but it sounds pretty horrible when it's put into words. I'm very fond of Lisa . . .

'Don't marry the girl out of pity!' exclaimed Helen quickly. 'That would be fatal—and it certainly wouldn't bring either of you happiness. Surely you must realize that? Do

194

you think Lisa is not sensitive enough to realize your motive—to resent it and to be hurt by it? Oh, Desmond, my dear, you know better than that!'

He rose abruptly, jolting the table by his unexpected movement. 'Sometimes it seems that I don't know anything,' he said bitterly, unhappily and strode away from her, Helen looked after him, her eyes troubled. She wished desperately that he could be ensured the happiness which he brought to so many people by his kindness and generosity and warm heart.

CHAPTER THIRTEEN

Isobel was surprised by Desmond's early arrival—and surprised even further to find that he was alone. He came around to the back of the house and entered the kitchen where he found Isobel preparing the midday meal, as he had expected.

Her fair hair was rumpled, her cheeks glowing from the heat of the oven and she was enveloped in a big white overall. Her sleeves were rolled up and she was making pastry on the kitchen table.

His heart lurched at sight of her and memories came flooding back—memories of a hot summer day when he had met Isobel for the first time and warmed to her fair loveliness, the warm friendliness and the natural ease with which she had accepted him.

He stood at the door and she remained motionless where she had turned from her task at his entry. They gazed into each other's eyes.

Then Isobel recovered her composure. 'You're early, Desmond,' she commented easily.

'Yes,' he admitted. 'I wanted to talk to you—so I left Helen and Ryan at the hotel and came over alone.'

At his words she caught her breath a little. 'Talk to me?' she repeated. The question was in her eyes and in her bearing as she turned to him.

He moved further into the kitchen and drew up a chair. Straddling it, he rested his arms on the wooden back. 'Go on with your work—what I have to say won't interrupt you very much.'

'I've almost finished,' she said automatically. 'Why not wait a few minutes, then we can talk in the sitting-room.'

He shook his head. 'I don't want Lisa to hear what I have to say,' he said.

She looked at him quickly. 'I can't imagine what you want to say that Lisa cannot hear,' she said slowly.

'Is she in the sitting-room?'

Isobel nodded. 'She's writing to Michael.'

Desmond's heart was racing wildly. His

courage was beginning to fail him. She was so lovely, so sweet—his lovely Isobel. He loved her so much. How could he deny the faintest chance of happiness—if only she had not promised to marry Frank Cummins. She was not married yet—there was no need for him to commit himself to Lisa. He could think of no better partner throughout life than this lovely woman with the shining grey eyes and aureole of fair hair.

There was a brief silence between them. Then Desmond took his courage in both hands. He thrust his chin up and faced Isobel squarely. 'I want to marry Lisa. Would you have any objections?' He was shocked to hear defiance in his tone. This was the last thing he wanted.

His words were so far removed from anything she had imagined he might say that she could only stare at him dumbly. Then, slowly, she bent down to pick up the knife she had dropped with a sharp clatter to the floor. She needed the momentary respite. Marry Lisa! Although she had hoped and worked for this, his wish came as a blow to her—and it was as though a knife had been driven into her heart right to the hilt. Pain and anguish swept through her body but she fought against it. This is what she had wanted for Lisa but she had not known that it would be like a death blow to her heart.

She turned back to her pastry, needing

something to concentrate on while she marshalled her reactions into some order. Automatically, she rolled out the pastry with deft, brisk movements.

The silence was too long. Desmond said gently, 'Well, Isobel? Don't you approve?'

She stumbled on her reply. 'If it's what you really want, Desmond—you sprung it on me so suddenly—I mean, of course I approve . . .' She broke off. What else could she do but give her blessing? The fulfilment of Lisa's dreams should surely fill her sister with happiness—but Isobel could only think at that moment of the shattering of her own happiness.

'Lisa loves me and I'm very fond of her,' he said awkwardly. 'I've thought about this for some weeks, Isobel—it's no snap decision. Do you think she would be happy?'

She looked at him, then afraid that her expression might give away her thoughts she turned back to her task, so that he only saw her profile. 'Are you in love with Lisa?' she asked and the question was a difficult one to speak.

Lisa, having heard the car draw up outside the house, wondered where its occupants were. Bowling her chair to the window, she recognized Desmond's car and realized that he and his friends must have gone around the house to the back door. She decided to go in search of the party, wondering why they had not come to the sitting-room. Pushing open the door, she bowled her chair into the hall and along the corridor. As she reached the kitchen door, which was slightly ajar, she heard Isobel's voice clearly and the question she was asking startled her. The rubber wheels of her chair made no sound on the hall floor and now she hesitated, wondering whether to make her presence known or whether to return as silently as she had come. She was not sly by nature and she had no wish to eavesdrop but her chair was difficult to turn round alone in the narrow hallway—and the mention of her own name was intriguing in itself.

Desmond replied after a brief hesitation: 'Isobel—how can you ask me that? You knew long ago how I felt—that you're the woman I love.'

Isobel's heart soared from the depths. She clasped her floury hands together as she spun round to face him. 'Then—why?'

'Because Lisa has a right to happiness. Because I know I can make her happy.' His reply was low but easily discernible to the paralysed girl in the wheelchair. A flush stained her cheeks and swift tears rushed to wet her lashes . . .

It did not occur to Isobel that Desmond knew nothing of Frank's decision to marry another woman. She seized only on the truth of his words that Lisa had more right to happiness than many another woman. She knew that it was not pity alone that stirred

Desmond. He was very fond of her: they were good friends and companions; he was kind and generous and Lisa would never find a better husband. Indeed, she might never find any husband if she did not marry Desmond. Few men would be prepared to take on a crippled wife, facing up to the difficulties of such a marriage, knowing she could never lead a normal married life or bear children. If Desmond could sacrifice the call of his heart and the love he knew for her, then surely Isobel could be as strong and as unselfish for Lisa's sake.

Isobel said slowly, 'Yes, you're right. You can make her happy, Desmond. She's been a different person since you came into our lives. She's radiant and whole—before she was always so alone, even with all the love that Michael and I could give her. Desperately alone—you and I can't imagine what it must be like. To be different from other people— never to walk down a country lane, or to swim in a sunlit pool, to dance and run and skip, to know the dew of the early morning when barefoot on the grass. But Lisa has never complained. She's always been gay and sunny and sweet. She loves you very much, Desmond. She's a single-minded person. There'll never be anyone else in her life but you. For her sake, I must agree to what you want—but take care of her, Desmond. Be good to her,' she pleaded with a break in her voice.

He nodded. 'She'll never regret anything—I promise you that much at least. I know the dreams she's always woven—I intend to see that most of them come true. All of them, if it's possible.'

Isobel said with a wealth of tenderness in her voice, 'And you, my dear? Will you be happy?'

Desmond shrugged. 'Isobel, once I wanted to marry you. You did not give me the chance to tell you so—but I'm sure you knew that I loved you. I've told myself since that I was wrong to believe my love was returned—for I think if you loved me, you'd have broken any promise you might have made to another man to find happiness with me. Until I found you, I thought I was self-sufficient—thought I needed no one in life. But we cannot marry— so I've turned my thoughts to Lisa. I've never known a woman as sweet, as innocent and as pure in mind and spirit as Lisa. I do love her, you know—not with the intensity and richness of the love I offered you—but enough to marry her and cherish her and never know any regret. Can you understand?'

Isobel said abruptly, 'You know that Lisa can never be a true wife to you?' It was difficult to speak of such things to him but she knew she must. She raised her hand and brushed her rumpled hair back from her brow. 'You understand that she'll never give you children? Surely it will be an unsatisfactory marriage for a man like you?'

'I know all these things. I still want to marry Lisa.' He met her eyes squarely. 'Only one woman has ever stirred my being completely—only one woman has ever known the entire depth of my love. That's you, Isobel—but if not you, then I'll marry Lisa. But I shall never want any woman but you in the way you mean. I feel very strongly that Lisa should know some happiness in life—and if I can ensure it, then I will.'

At this point, Lisa could bear no more. She leaned forward and pushed open the kitchen door. She wheeled herself into the room. Desmond and Isobel turned sharply towards her and their eyes were instinctively guarded. Desmond rose to his feet. Lisa looked from one to the other with tears in her eyes. But she was smiling—a tremulous smile. She raised a hand and brushed the tears from her lashes.

'They say that listeners never hear any good of themselves,' she said quietly. 'How untrue that is!'

'You heard—everything?' Isobel asked quickly.

'Not everything,' Lisa replied evenly. 'But enough. You're a pair of darling fools.'

Desmond moved quickly to her side and took her hands. 'Lisa, listen to me. You must have heard me telling Isobel that I want to marry you. I do, really I do. Whatever else you heard, discount it. The most important thing is that I want to marry you.' He spoke fervently, emotionally.

Lisa shook her head. 'I love you, Desmond,' she said very gently. 'You know that full well. I'm not sorry—I'm glad. It's a wonderful thing to love someone—even if you can never share their life. I'll never marry you, Desmond.' She released one of her hands and held it out to Isobel. Isobel moved forward and took it between both her hands. 'You've always sacrificed yourself for me, Isobel,' Lisa added with love in her voice. 'But I won't accept this sacrifice on your part, no matter how willing you are to make it. I've always known that you and Desmond love each other—I'm glad that it should be so. I want you both to be very happy.'

'Darling, think what it would mean to be Desmond's wife,' Isobel urged her sister.

Lisa smiled. 'I have thought—and I know it's impossible for me. But not for you, Isobel. Have you really thought what it would mean to give him up completely? To go through life without him when you both need each other so much?' She turned to Desmond. 'I heard you say something about Isobel making a promise to another man—did she mean Frank Cummins? Did she tell you that she was going to marry Frank?'

He nodded. 'Yes—but this was months ago. I reconciled myself to life without her—but I need you, Lisa. Don't let me down. Say that you'll marry me—I swear I'll make you happy. I'll never regret it—you'll never hear me say that I wish I'd married Isobel ...'

'But you'd always think it,' she said gently. 'Hasn't Isobel told you that Frank is engaged to another woman—that she had never promised herself to him. It was just one of those things that sometimes happen. We've known Frank all our lives. He's always been fond of Isobel—I used to tease her that one day he'd ask her to marry him.' She squeezed Isobel's fingers. 'If she told you such a thing, Desmond—it was because of me. She knew I cared for you—she was being noble. Can't you see that?'

Desmond looked at Isobel with a question in his eyes. 'Well, Isobel?'

She sighed. 'It's true.'

'Then you've always loved me?' he asked eagerly.

'Of course she has!' Lisa put in quickly. 'Thank you for wanting to marry me, Desmond—I know exactly why you turned to me. I would have known even if I hadn't overheard your conversation. My answer would have been the same—thank you but it's impossible.' She smiled up at Isobel. 'You've a right to happiness too, Isobel—you've always put Michael and me before everything else. It's time that you were selfish in a good cause. If you marry Desmond, I shall be the first one to give my blessing—and it won't alter my love for both of you in the least.' She released her hands. 'I'm going back to the sitting-room. You won't want an audience for the next few minutes.'

Without a word, Desmond bent down and kissed her lips, gently and with real warmth. Then Lisa turned her chair and went from the room. She did not return to the sitting-room. She went into her small, nun-like bedroom and picked up a book that lay beside her bed. It always lay on the table, open at one page. With very real pain in her heart, Lisa read the lines which she treasured so much:

> 'Never shall I leave again
> My lady in her cloak
> Of fair and shining beauty
> When I return from wanderings abroad . . .'

Desmond had come to claim his lady and there would be no more wanderings abroad for him. Gradually, the pain abated and in its place came calm acceptance and the looking forward to a future in which she would know a quiet contentment in the happiness of Isobel and Desmond.

Desmond turned to Isobel. 'The purity of her soul puts mine to shame,' he said in a low voice. 'Now what do we do?'

She smiled at him. 'Exactly what Lisa says— I know my sister. She will never retract her decision—and we mustn't spoil the generosity of her actions, Desmond.'

Their eyes met and at last Isobel did not have to guard her expression. In her eyes he read the shining truth of her love for him and her mouth curved with a sweetness that brought him pain with its very beauty. He cradled her lovely face in his hands and gently touched her lips—the kiss was light and tender and spoke more of the wealth of devotion he offered than any amount of passion or warmth could have done.

He took her into the curve of his arm and she rested her head against his heart. He looked down at the crisp golden aureole, the tender curve of her cheek and he was filled with a love that was akin to adoration.

'Then you will marry me, Isobel?' His words were a plea.

She nodded and held him close. 'I love you, Desmond—so very much. I want to spend the rest of my life with you.'

They kissed again and time stood still.

Then he drew away a little and said, 'But what of Lisa? If only there were some way to make her happy.' He sighed softly.

'The only other thing Lisa wants from life is to be able to walk,' Isobel replied quietly. 'That has always been her dream—above everything else, I know.'

He made up his mind with swift determination.

'Then we'll have to do something about

that. I won't accept the impossibility of it, Isobel. It's a good many years since she saw a specialist, isn't it? Science is always making progress. She shall see new specialists—the best in the world. I don't care what it costs—if it's possible to give her an active life, then she shall have it.'

'I've been putting money aside for a long time,' Isobel told him. 'As much as I could. There's a man in Rome who's working miracles with people in Lisa's position. I've been saving to take her to Italy so that he could see her. If he had given me the slightest hope, then I would have done everything possible to afford an operation for her.' She added quietly, 'If necessary, I'd have sold the house—against my father's wishes. In his will, he made a proviso that the house must never go out of our hands—but he didn't leave us much money for its maintenance.' She sighed.

'Why didn't you tell me about this Italian?' he demanded. 'You knew I'd help. I'll gladly send Lisa to Rome—and pay for the operation.'

'How could I ask you? You've already done so much for us. Michael's school fees, your kindness to us all, your friendship—all these things. We can never hope to repay you for that, let alone the cost of Lisa's trip to Rome or the operation.'

He tilted her chin. 'My darling, knowing that you love me is all the reward I want—or shall ever want. As my wife, your family is my responsibility—now and always. You'll marry me soon, won't you?'

'I can't leave Lisa,' she demurred. 'If she's cured, I'll marry you immediately.'

'Whether the operation is successful or not, you'll marry me as soon as Lisa comes back from Rome,' he told her masterfully. 'Lisa is always sure of a home with us.' He began to make plans. 'We'll keep on the London flat. It will be useful. I'll buy a house in Kent for us all. But we'll keep this house, of course.'

Isobel looked up at him, her eyes shining. 'Do you realize that if Lisa is cured—if she can lead a normal life—it opens up a world of possibilities. She might easily meet someone who can make her happy. She'll never love anyone as she loves you—but there are different degrees of love. She might even marry and have children. Oh, Desmond—the future seems so bright and wonderful.'

'It is, my darling.' He caught her close.

'Is it right to take so much from you?' she asked slowly. 'I'm not sure if I should let you send Lisa to Rome.'

'It would be terribly wrong of you to refuse,' he told her gently. 'Lisa has given up her own happiness for us—we must try to bring her another kind of happiness. You know so much more than I do what it would mean to her— you've no right to refuse an opportunity like this, Isobel,' He kissed her fair hair. 'You've no right to deny me the joy of giving, either.'

'I never thought there was so much joy in the world,' she murmured, caressing his cheek with her long, slender fingers. He caught her fingers in his hand and held them to his lips. He smiled down at her, at peace and rich in the knowledge that his lovely Isobel was going to be his wife and share his life.

'Tell me about this man—this spinal specialist?' he asked.

'His name is Brocco and he has a private nursing home in Rome. He has already done many operations on apparently hopeless cases. He cured five completely: the others can walk a little but still lead a fairly inactive life. The five he cured were claimed as miracles by the Italian press. I wrote to the specialist who has examined Lisa occasionally since she was a child—and he sent me full particulars of Brocco's work with the hope that he could do something for Lisa if I could afford to send her to Italy. He offered to contact Brocco himself and give him full details of Lisa's case.'

'Well, that will be useful. You must give me more details later, darling, and I'll make arrangements for the journey. You'll go with Lisa, of course. I'll travel with you but I shall have to come back to England. It's likely to be a long business, you know. It isn't just a question of an operation—Lisa's likely to be at the nursing home for months even if Brocco isn't successful.'

'I realize that,' Isobel replied. 'How soon will she be able to go to Italy?'

'That depends on Brocco, I suppose. I hope it won't be too long,' he said quietly. 'I'm impatient for my wife, darling.'

'As soon as we come back from Italy,' she promised.

He nodded. 'Yes, that's a reasonable promise, Isobel. You needn't worry about Michael—if you're still away when his holidays come round, I'll have him with me in London. Maybe we'll both fly over to Italy to see you for a little while.' He smiled down at Isobel. 'I think of Michael rather in the light of a son, you know.'

'I hope we'll have sons of our own,' she said shyly.

He drew her to him, touched by the expression of his own hopes. They clung together, lost in the wonder of their mutual love.

When Desmond released her, Isobel said eagerly, 'We must tell Lisa. Let's go to her now, Desmond.'

He nodded. 'But don't fill her up with too many hopes, my dearest. It could turn out to be a great disappointment—and that would be a bitter blow to her.'

'I've never told her about Brocco—or that I've been saving money in the hope that he could help her. But there's no need to worry, Desmond. Lisa will understand that there is only the merest hope that she'll walk after the operation—indeed, she'll probably accept the unlikelihood of success without question. Then she will be all the more overjoyed if Brocco cures her. Lisa is that kind of person.'

Lisa was stunned at first by the news: then came overwhelming gratitude to Desmond which swept away the last trace of sadness in her soul that her love for him was in vain; lastly came the quiet acceptance which Isobel had forecast.

She was very patient during the next few months while Desmond was in touch with Brocco and making the necessary arrangements. She rarely spoke of the coming ordeal—she knew it would be an ordeal for Desmond had warned her that a great deal of pain would accompany the operation which was still largely experimental, despite Brocco's past successes.

Ryan Nesbit came down to the little white house to begin the portrait of Lisa. In time, this portrait was known as the best of his works and it brought him both fame and success beyond his wildest dreams.

Ryan and Lisa were always together. When he was not working, he sought her company and they talked and laughed together. Isobel felt that Ryan was the best tonic Lisa could have had during these waiting months, although too she sometimes felt that her sister no longer needed her now that she had Ryan.

There was a closeness between them. But she was not afraid for either Ryan or Lisa. She knew Ryan loved Helen with a deep devotion and that nothing would ever change his emotions. She knew too that Ryan had come into their lives at a time when Lisa, sacrificing her own dreams, had needed someone like him to make her heart lighter.

Ryan was very happy: he worked hard and found contentment in his surroundings; he found great joy in the friendship with Lisa and Isobel. He could look forward to a future which held great promise and he knew that he had a lot for which to thank Desmond Crane. Yet Desmond was a man who would never want such thanks. He found great pleasure in helping his fellow men in the ways that presented themselves.

Desmond did not explain to his friends that it was Isobel who would eventually be his wife and not Lisa. They knew of his plans to send Lisa to Italy and therefore were sure that they understood his generous motives. Only Lisa knew that Isobel would marry Desmond when they returned from Italy and she only spoke of these plans to her sister.

The portrait was finally completed a few days before they left for Italy. Ryan had never known such satisfaction with his own work and he said as much to Desmond.

Desmond stood back and surveyed the portrait. He had the eye of a connoisseur and he said: 'This is ten times better than I expected, Ryan, and I had complete faith in your genius. I'm glad you're pleased with your efforts. There is always one time in an artist's life when something he has accomplished comes near to giving complete satisfaction. But of course a true artist strives for the perfection that only he feels is possible—and never really achieves in his own eyes.' He turned and smiled at his friend. 'This is better than an insurance office, eh?'

'Definitely! ' Ryan replied fervently. 'Thank God I had the opportunity.'

'Thank God for your gift,' Desmond replied quietly. 'This proves how right you were to recognize your star and follow it at whatever cost to yourself or anyone else.'

'Everyone has a star in life—but not everyone is fortunate enough to reach it,' the artist returned.

Thinking of Isobel and how near he had been to losing her, Desmond silently agreed. He would have been content to follow his star for ever without the hope of attaining it—but now that it was within his grasp, he knew that his destiny was about to be fulfilled.

CHAPTER FOURTEEN

Desmond scanned the sky for the first sign of the aeroplane. In the far distance the sun glinted on a silver bird and he turned to Helen eagerly. 'There she is—it won't be long now.'

'You must be anxious to see them again,' she said smiling.

He nodded. 'I only wish I could have flown over to bring them home. But as Ryan's sponsor, I could scarcely not be present at the opening of his first exhibition.' He grinned at Ryan who stood beside him, his arm about Michael. He was talking to the boy about the airport and the various planes. Desmond had brought Michael down from Scotland several weeks ago at the beginning of his summer holiday. Ryan had made friends with him when Michael returned home at Christmas and found the artist busy on his sister's portrait. He loved and understood children and Desmond could not suppress an occasional flicker of jealousy that Michael had so readily given his boyish affections to another man.

The exhibition that Desmond mentioned had opened the previous day and contained Lisa's portrait as its centrepiece, surrounded by many other of Ryan's works—some done before he had ever heard of Desmond Crane or met him—others since he had finished

Lisa's portrait. They were all excellent but none came up to the standard of this portrait which had that morning been acclaimed in the press as one of the greatest works of art of the generation.

The silver bird came nearer and arced above the airport, seeming to hover indefinitely before it slowly approached the landing field.

Desmond could hardly contain his impatience. It was two months since he had flown over for a brief week-end with Isobel and Lisa and missing Isobel was an intolerable ache which he carried with him all the time. But now they were home and in his breast pocket he carried a special license which would enable him to marry Isobel at the earliest opportunity. He knew she was as impatient as he and he wondered now at her feelings as the aeroplane taxied slowly across the field before coming to a standstill.

They waited as the silver airway steps were set against the side of the aeroplane and the door opened. Airport officials hurried up the steps and entered.

It seemed an interminable wait before the passengers began to leave and Desmond scanned each person as they came down to the fresh green earth again. Then he caught the glint of sunlight on golden hair and saw the slim figure of Isobel in the doorway. His heart lifted and he moved instinctively towards the gateway through which the passengers came.

Helen linked her arm in Ryan's and they followed him, Michael at their side, proud of Ryan's possessive arm about his shoulders.

It was an incredible joy to see Lisa walking, a little unsteadily to be sure, but walking across the grass towards the little group that waited, Isobel at her side, anxious for each step. Her face was bright with eagerness.

At sight of Desmond's welcoming figure, Lisa quickened her pace and then, a few yards away from him, she ran into his arms. He held her close while she clung to him, speechless with happiness. Then she lifted her face and he kissed her.

'Welcome home, my dear,' he murmured— but he looked over her bright head into the beloved face of Isobel. She stood, waiting, a tremulous smile on her lips—and he read in her eyes all that he longed to know.

'Isn't it wonderful!' Lisa cried. 'I begged Signor Brocco to let me come home without a wheelchair—he was dubious but I promised that I wouldn't tire myself.'

'I can't believe it yet,' Desmond told her happily. 'I knew you'd made wonderful progress—but I never expected this.'

'There's months yet before she can really go wild,' Isobel said quietly. 'She'll have to rest for days now—but in time she'll be as active as you or I, Desmond.'

He released Lisa and stood back, surveying

the slight figure in the blue dress. 'This is the first time I've seen you on your feet—two months ago you were flat on your back.'

She laughed up at him. 'I never knew how hard it was to walk,' she told him. 'I felt as helpless as a baby—I kept falling over at first. Signor Brocco was so patient with me.'

'I didn't expect you to be so small,' he said lightly. 'Why, Isobel is taller than you are—and she's only a shrimp.'

Suddenly he remembered his friends. He turned round to look for them and they approached, 'We thought we'd give you a moment alone,' Helen said. 'Lisa, my dear—how well you look and how wonderful to see you walk so well!'

Michael flung himself upon Lisa. 'Why didn't you tell me?' he demanded. 'You never said a word in your letters. Isn't it marvellous, Ryan?' he turned to the artist. 'Lisa can actually walk now.'

Ryan laid a steadying hand on the boy's shoulder. 'Don't bowl her over, Michael. 'You're quite a heavy weight you know.' He smiled into Lisa's eyes. 'You're lovelier than ever, Lisa,' he said and the admiration in his eyes carried more weight than his words.

She lifted her bare arms. 'Look at the tan,' she said. 'Italy's a wonderful place. So much sun—and the people are charming.'

Helen turned to Isobel who stood a little outside the excited group. 'How nice to see

217

you again,' she said. 'You're looking very well, too.'

'It's good to be back in England again,' Isobel said. 'I loved Italy but it's a long time to be away from familiar things.'

'But worth it all for Lisa's sake. I cannot get over the complete success of the operation—Brocco must be a marvellous surgeon.'

'He is,' Isobel said sincerely.

The others greeted her in due course—all but Desmond who had not yet spoken to her directly. She understood. She had wished that their meeting could have been private and intimate—but she had been content to let Lisa take the limelight.

At last they left the airport, Desmond attending to all the necessary formalities and sending the rest of the party on to his big car.

Lisa made no complaint but from the thankful way she sat down in the back of the car it was apparent that it had been quite an effort to walk from the reception hall to the car. They talked generalities until Desmond joined them. The big car soon ate up the miles to London. On the way they discussed in full Lisa's miraculous recovery. The operation had been long and arduous and at one point it had been touch and go whether she would survive it. But despite her air of fragility, she had a strong constitution and, above all, the will to live and to walk. Humorously, she described her first attempts at walking and added that

218

she had never expected it to be such an effort to put one foot before the other and keep upright and balanced.

'It may be a perfectly natural thing for an infant,' she said lightly, 'but at twenty-two it's an ordeal.'

They talked too about Ryan's exhibition at the Bond Street gallery and Lisa said that her first outing would be to view it. She added that she longed to listen to the comments of the public on Ryan's work—but it would be difficult to restrain herself from boasting that he was a great friend and that she was the subject of the main portrait.

'They'll recognize you immediately,' Desmond assured her. 'The portrait has been reproduced in all the major newspapers—the whole of England is familiar with your face by now, my dear.'

They went directly to Helen's flat. It had been arranged that Isobel and Lisa should stay with her for the time being while Michael continued to stay with Desmond.

Coffee was served immediately on their arrival. Desmond had insisted on carrying Lisa in his arms from the car and now she was lying on a comfortable settee with Ryan in attendance. Helen excused herself from the lounge and went to check that the bedrooms were in order for Lisa and Isobel. Michael sat on a low stool at Lisa's side and was as concerned for her well-being as Ryan, who plied her with coffee and sandwiches and conversation.

Isobel went to stand by the window. She was a little weary, more from reaction than the length of the journey which had been comparatively easy. After a few moments, Desmond joined her. He stood beside her, not touching her, not even looking at her—but both were conscious of the glow radiating from the other.

'My darling,' he murmured. 'I've missed you so much, Isobel.'

She smiled, her lips curving in sweetness. 'It's all over now, Desmond—I'll never go away again. Thank God that Lisa is well and active again.'

He turned and looked at Lisa who was bubbling over with happiness and excitement, talking eagerly to Ryan and Michael, more youthful than Desmond had ever known her to be. The change in her was astonishing. The serenity remained in her quieter moments and the purity of her innocence still shone from her eyes. But she was alive and vital, enjoying life to the full, and she was talking now of her plans for the future.

'Thank God!' he repeated fervently. 'Now we'll never need to reproach ourselves, Isobel. We took away one happiness—but we gave her a much better gift—the ability to be a normal woman and know all the pleasures of life.'

Now he turned his gaze upon Isobel and she

looked up at him. No smile on her lips now. A steadfast gaze which told him that there was to be no more waiting, that his love had returned, ready and more than willing to be his wife.

He tapped his breast pocket. 'I have the license,' he said. In their frequent letters to one another, they had planned the future to the last detail. 'When, Isobel?'

She smiled. 'A few days. We must give Lisa time to recover from the journey. She'll never forgive us if she isn't at the wedding, you know.'

'A few days,' he agreed. 'That will give me time to show you the house I'd like to buy. It's twenty minutes from London in the car. I wouldn't close the deal until you'd seen the house, darling. It must be a house you like and where you'll be happy, Isobel.'

'Anywhere—with you,' she said gently.

He took her hand and squeezed it. 'Be careful—if you say things like that, I shall kiss you now—and to hang with everyone else.'

'Did you finally tell Helen and Ryan that you're marrying me—and not Lisa?'

He nodded. 'I thought they'd be surprised but Helen merely said that she had known all along that you were the one I really wanted. She's so pleased that you finally agreed to marry me, bless her!'

'And Ryan?'

'His first thought was for Lisa but when I told him that Lisa knew and understood the circumstances, he gave his blessing.'

Isobel nodded. She said quietly, 'You know, darling, Ryan is the one man I should like to see married to Lisa. They're such wonderful friends and I know they're fond of each other.'

'You're forgetting Helen,' he said slowly. 'She's been very patient and I hope that they'll be married soon now.' There was a trace of anxiety in his voice.

She laughed a little. 'Desmond, my dear, how concerned you always are with other people's happiness.' She sobered instantly. 'I only hope you're going to find it with me, my darling.'

He slipped his arm about her shoulders and drew her close to him. She gazed up at him. 'Can you doubt it?' he whispered against her hair. 'You told me once that the future is very bright—it would be nothing without you, Isobel. Some men seek all their lives in vain, for the promise that you offer me now.' As he looked into her lovely face he smiled and his eyes were bright with love. At that moment, Lisa called across to them.

'Desmond, do you remember that poem—"Never shall I leave again"? Hasn't it been rather reversed now? It's Isobel who has returned "from wanderings abroad".'

His arm tightened about Isobel's shoulders. 'Yes, and this time she's with me for good.' He lowered his voice until his words were for Isobel's ears alone. 'My lady of fair and shining beauty,' he said gently. 'My beloved star . . .'

They were married a few days later, as Isobel had promised. It was a quiet wedding in a small church in a London square.

Trembling, not with nervousness but with joy, Isobel made her responses and Desmond slipped his ring on her finger. They exchanged a glance of such pure love and joy that Lisa, her eyes upon them, knew beyond doubt that she had been right to insist upon this marriage. Her own love for Desmond was untarnished but it was because of her love that she could witness his wedding to her sister without a tear or an ache in her heart. She would never love again with such intensity but Lisa knew that her life had been altered completely by the operation. The future held many a promise and perhaps one day she would meet a man whom she could love enough to marry. For the moment, the present joys of life were sufficient but eventually she would want the fulfilment of marriage. An affection like that she felt for Ryan, a friendship such as they shared, a mental and spiritual harmony mingled with physical attraction as existed between herself and Ryan—if there were a man who could stir her to these things in the future, then she would accept the less bright star and know happiness if not the deep joy which she could have known with Desmond.

As they came out of the church, the sun dazzled them with its brilliance after the somewhat subdued interior of the church.

Gaily, Ryan, Helen and Lisa pelted them with rose petals and confetti, to the amusement of the few who had gathered to watch the wedding party leave the church. Michael was stealthily employed in attaching an old boot to the back of the car and a large placard on which he had laboriously painted the words 'Just Married'.

Laughing and holding hands, Desmond and Isobel hurriedly stepped into the car and slammed the door on their well-wishers.

The car drew away and they looked back to see waving hands and smiling faces. Isobel shook out the soft folds of her short dress and a shower of confetti fell to the floor. She turned to her husband and brushed his shoulders. He laughed. 'Leave it,' he told her and drew her into his arms. 'Be a dutiful wife and kiss your husband.'

'As if I need telling,' she chided him and raised her face to his.

They had planned a small reception at Helen's flat and then they were going away for a short honeymoon—to the little white house where on a day similar to this, with the sun shining down benevolently, they had first met.

As they stepped from the car, Desmond brushed confetti from his suit. He gave his man directions to garage the car and then come up to the flat to drink their healths. As the car drew away, Desmond noticed the boot and the placard.

'So that's why Michael was so pleased with himself, the little wretch!' he exclaimed. 'I wondered what he was keeping up his sleeve.'

'I expect he was aided and abetted by Ryan,' Isobel said laughingly.

They were admitted into the flat by Helen's maid who then discreetly left them alone. Desmond took the opportunity to kiss his bride thoroughly. She gave herself up to the wonders of his endearments and embraces. It was all too short for the others had been close behind them in another car.

The reception was lively and gay, high-spirited. At last, Desmond and Isobel made their escape much to the regret of Lisa and Michael and their friends.

With Isobel by his side, Desmond whistled softly to himself as the car sped along the dusty, country roads. The sun shone from a blue sky and the surrounding fields and hedges were green and pleasant. It was a very hot day. Desmond had decided to take the sports car and the hood was down. The sunshine was warm and welcome on their bare heads.

The car ate up the miles with ease. He switched on the radio and soft music floated out on to the warm air. He turned his head and smiled at Isobel who sat very close to him, her hand on his knee, her other hand with the bright wedding ring encircling her finger lying in her lap.

They were almost to the house when the smooth-running engine suddenly caught and spluttered. A frown creased his brow. He slowed down and again the engine caught. His petrol gauge informed him that it was not the fault of an empty tank.

'That's strange,' he murmured, slowing down to a standstill. 'I'd better have a look at the engine.'

'Be careful of your clothes, darling,' Isobel warned him automatically.

He grinned. 'The wifely touch already?' He got out and pushed up the bonnet. Carefully he investigated the engine. He soon found the fault but it was nothing he could remedy. He began to laugh lightly and he came back to Isobel. Leaning on the door, he said, 'History repeats itself—or this is where I came in. Sorry, darling, we'll have to walk the rest of the way—this is a fine beginning to our honeymoon. I should have had the car overhauled but it slipped my mind with so many other things to arrange.'

'It isn't very far,' she assured him. 'We'll stop at Frank's farm and use his telephone—he won't mind.'

He nodded and helped her from the car. He put his arm about her shoulders. 'I am sorry about this, Isobel. Those shoes are scarcely the thing for walking on dusty roads—you'll be so hot, too.'

She strained on her toes to kiss his lips

lightly. 'I'm a country girl, remember. I'm used to walking—and the shoes will stand up to it. Anyway, it's rather fun—it's certainly an unusual way to start a honeymoon!'

They began to walk. 'The ways of destiny are very strange,' Desmond said lightly. 'I never thought I'd meet my future wife when I last walked along this road—I certainly never thought that you and I would be walking it together on our wedding day!'

Green fields rolled away on both sides: the long road stretched before and beyond. The countryside was as beautiful and as desolate as any plain. In the far distance a low range of hills outlined the horizon.

They had not walked very far before they heard the sound of a car engine behind them. Turning, they saw an old Ford car rattling along the road.

'It's Frank!' Isobel exclaimed.

It was indeed Frank and he pulled up at sight of them. 'Is that your car stranded back there?' he asked. 'Hallo, Isobel—how are you? Hallo, Crane. Can I give you a lift?'

Simultaneously, they said, 'No, thanks. We'd rather walk.' At the sound of their happy voices in chorus, they exchanged happy glances and laughed.

'I'm going to the village—I'll tell Bert Stoner what's happened and get him to drive out and take a look at the car.'

After a few more minutes, he drove on.

227

'Nice chap!' Desmond commented. 'Is he married yet?'

'Some months ago,' Isobel replied.

He tightened his arm about her shoulders. 'I'm glad you didn't mention that we were married today, darling.'

She looked up quickly. 'Why, it never occurred to me! I suppose I'm not used to the idea myself yet.'

They rounded a corner of the road and saw the house. The small white house set back from the road with the narrow lane leading to it. It merged with the countryside and, despite its lonely position, had an air of wholeness and welcome.

Bright curtains fluttered from open windows. They pushed open the gate and walked up the path, looking about them. During the week, Isobel had travelled down to set the place in order. While she was away, a village woman had kept her eye on the house and given it a thorough spring-clean just before Isobel and Lisa returned to England.

They paused on the threshold and Isobel raised her shining eyes to his face. 'Welcome home, my darling,' she said softly. Her eyes were clear and bright—of a beauty so rare that love surged in his heart for his woman—and he felt himself drowning in their depths.

Without a word, he took a key from his pocket and inserted it in the door. Swinging the door wide, he paused a moment then turning to Isobel, he caught her up in his arms and carried her over the threshold. As they entered the cool interior of the house, he knew that they crossed more than the threshold of a house—they crossed the threshold into a new life and a new happiness.

We hope you have enjoyed this Large Print book. Other Chivers Press or Thorndike Press Large Print books are available at your library or directly from the publishers.

For more information about current and forthcoming titles, please call or write, without obligation, to:

Chivers Press Limited
Windsor Bridge Road
Bath BA2 3AX
England
Tel. (01225) 335336

OR

G.K. Hall & Co.
295 Kennedy Memorial Drive
Waterville
Maine 04901
USA

All our Large Print titles are designed for easy reading, and all our books are made to last.